STRIPPER NOIR

by

Armand Rosamilia and Erin Louis

A HellBound Books LLC Publication

Printed in the USA

Armand Rosamilia and Erin Louis

STRIPPER NOIR

Chapter One

What happens in Vegas stays in Vegas, especially if it involves strippers and murder.

Especially if it involves strippers being murdered, and women you are quite fond of.

Frank Michi knew hanging out in strip clubs all day and night was not conducive to getting his life back in order, but right now… he needed another rum and Coke.

Cinnamon, whose real name was Cammi, was busy with a group of businessmen in crooked ties and untucked shirts, enjoying a late lunch and getting loaded. The other end of the bar was packed with the typical daytime crowd: big spenders sneaking out of the office to ogle some pretty women and hand over the loose bills in their wallet before having to get home to the once-pretty wife and their brain-dead kids, all juiced up on videogames and the boob tube.

Frank was not only a judge of character, he loved to judge everyone around him and see where he fell on that particular bar. He usually fell well under it. Even some of the low-lives who spent their days and nights in casinos and strip clubs in this particular Sin City had it better than he ever would.

Coulda had it all, Frank thought and frowned. *Coulda been a contender.*

He was about to lean over the bar and get his own refill when the door opened, a brief flash of sunlight trying to race across the dimly lit room and maybe touch some skin on the stage. It fell a few feet short before everyone was plunged back into blue and purple false light, strobing continuously. It always gave Frank a headache if he sat here too long, and even though he'd been coming to this particular club since The Incident, he still hadn't found the perfect seat.

What caused him to frown even deeper was what had wandered into the strip club: his ex-partner.

Frank put his head down and stared into the empty glass, praying Tyler Fitt didn't notice him. They'd gone through the Academy together, graduating one and two, and been paired from day one. They'd had a bond. It went beyond normal cop stuff. It was a genuine friendship. They'd both hung out on their days off. Double dated their wives. Been one another's best man, although Tyler was still happily married and Frank was happily divorced.

The cop with Tyler looked like a baby right out of the Academy, wearing an ill-fitting suit from Sears or JC Penney. He didn't have the stare all cops working in this town got, but he'd get it soon enough.

Tyler was talking to one of the bouncers, who nodded and walked away. Likely to get his boss. Frank knew something was up. This wasn't two guys going to get a beer and see some hot chicks vying for their cash. This was definitely police business.

Frank looked away a second too late, and Tyler locked eyes with him. Frank groaned inside. He didn't want his old partner and friend to see him like this, although lately there was no other way to see him. If he wasn't spending his last twenty on beer and wandering two blocks to his seedy apartment, there'd be nowhere else to find him.

"You look like the cat dragged you in," Tyler said. He shook his head. "Actually, you look like the cat had a hairball named Frank and puked you up."

Frank smiled faintly. "Great to see you, too, Fitt."

"Is this coincidence I'm finding you here?" Tyler asked. "You know there's been a murder."

"Here?" Frank caught Cinnamon's eye and tapped on his empty mug. "Buy me a round or two and tell me all about it."

"I'm on duty."

"Never stopped us before," Frank said. "We used to enjoy our liquid lunches. Helped us to see well. Sink down to the dirtbag level and catch the bad guys."

"Some of us never pulled ourselves back from that level," Frank said quietly. He leaned on the bar next to Frank, blocking his new partner. "You need help, old friend."

"I need a beer and..." Frank winked at Cinnamon as she placed a cold mug on the bar. "Presto. I have a beer. What else do you need in life?"

"You lost your focus. I worry about you." Tyler glanced over his shoulder. "This kid is nice and all but I miss the real action with you. We made a difference in this town."

Frank snorted. "We did a lot of things that crossed the line, too. All in the name of justice and liberty."

"I wish it hadn't ended the way it did for you."

Frank shrugged. "But it did. Water under the bridge." He took a sip of beer and smacked his lips. "I'm fine. I get my exercise. I eat when I'm hungry. I enjoy the view from this chair."

"If you need anything, please get in touch," Tyler said. "My number hasn't changed."

"I lost my phone a while ago and found out I didn't need it anymore." Frank took another sip but grabbed his former partner by the arm when he turned away. "Tell me about this murder."

Tyler turned back and squinted. Frank could see his new partner was antsy, eyes everywhere and not just on the flesh writhing onstage to a Whitesnake tune.

"Cassandra Sasevich was killed in the back parking lot after midnight," Tyler said. "If you frequent this place you'd know her as K.C. Sass."

Frank nodded. "I knew her. Pretty girl. Young, too. She didn't have the look some of these women get after a while."

"What look?"

"You know what I'm talking about. A few get hooked on the drugs, either actual drugs or the lure of the money. The grab of men wanting them so badly they dump their wallets out for a lap dance. It is as intoxicating as the beer or the cocaine."

Tyler sighed. "You got anything on your mind I should know about?"

Frank shook his head. "Just know what you already know, buddy. It was good seeing you."

After Tyler left, Frank finished his beer and tipped Cinnamon. He'd decided it was time to go home. Sleep another day off. K.C. Sass wasn't exactly a daughter to Frank, but she was family. All of the girls were family, since it was all he had left in this world that wasn't tainted.

Only, now it was. Now one of them was dead.

Frank wasn't surprised to notice Tyler following him as he made his way from the strip club to his apartment. He didn't think he was a person of interest, but Tyler had to know Frank was holding back. Playing it close to the vest. He'd want to eliminate Frank as a suspect so he could move on, and if he could pry some much-needed information out of his former partner, so much the better.

Chapter Two

Fucking Whitesnake again. I'm going to have to have another conversation with Mike,

Minnie thought as she watched two very obvious detectives approach Frank, a frequent customer. She was fond of Frank but tried not to spend too much time with him. He was very obviously depressed but had only spoken vaguely about the reason why. He was one of the locals, and while a friendly face was welcome on a slow shift, he wasn't much good for lap dances.

As she waited for the hopelessly cheesy song to be over, Minnie was keeping a close eye from the stage on the two men talking to Frank. It looked like he knew them. Minnie was aware of Frank's prior occupation, but was unable to discern whether this was a friendly conversation or not. Minnie had no doubt this visit from the cops was about Sass's murder. She was annoyed at the interest the police had, but at the same time, a little touched. At least they gave a shit this time. Most of the time, when a "lady of the night" went missing or was killed, no one cared. Least of all the cops. That was of course why they kept going missing and murdered.

"Let's give it up for Venus, our own red hot redheaded goddess," Mike finally said in his sleazy cocaine-induced raspy voice.

Minnie collected her tips, and sauntered off the stage. She was about to walk to the sound booth to gently remind the half drunk DJ that Whitesnake sucked ass and she would prefer if he stuck to her list of songs, but decided that the conversation with Mike could wait. After all, it was unlikely he'd remember anyway. Frank had left, with the two detectives following shortly after. Minnie needed to know why.

Minnie, short for Minerva, was named after the Greek goddess of wisdom. She used Venus as her stripper name, not only because it was a common and forgettable stripper name, but because it was the name of the Greek goddess of love and sex.

With her flaming red hair and light blue eyes, Minnie was just attractive enough to make a handsome living as a stripper, but just ordinary enough to go unnoticed if she wanted to. Drop dead average if you will.

Versatility was keys to both her profession and her extra-curricular activities. Right now, the latter was more of her concern.

Cassandra aka KC Sass, was a sometime friend of Minnie's. A young girl equipped with enough intelligence to have had a bright future ahead of her, stripper or not, but still very naive.

Naivety in the Las Vegas strip club scene could prove dangerous, even deadly. Minnie was saddened by her murder, but also highly pissed about it. Cassandra had her faults, but her death was a tragedy.

Minnie had a complicated relationship with many of her colleagues. Most of the time she found them shallow and annoying. She had few friends, if any at all, and none of them close.

Minnie found a good portion of her counterparts to be good-hearted, sometimes damaged, and all around decent human beings.

Cassandra fell into this category. Sweet and kind but starting to develop a fondness for liquor, which Minnie thought might be a slippery slope. Minnie kept an eye on her, ready to help guide Cassandra back on track if need be… but she also kept her distance.

The other portion of her coworkers, thankfully not as common as the first, are women who could best be described as predators.

These women prey on the weak. Not only their customers, but other women as well. These women predators rob, manipulate, and in some cases actually murder their clients if it served their agendas. These women made things difficult for the hard working women in the adult entertainment business, and it was Minnie's mission to stop them. Even if it meant stooping to their level.

Feigning a headache, Minnie paid out her stage fee and tips, dressed and left her shift a little early. Having secured a respectable reputation with the staff, she was granted much more leeway than most of the other girls. She got in her car and drove back to her home on the outskirts of town.

Jeff greeted her as she walked into her sparsely furnished but elegant apartment. He had a look of contempt on his face which she had long since stopped taking personally. The bottom of his food dish was slightly visible. As a cat, looks of disdain and contempt were kind of his thing. "Well, fuck you too," she said as she refilled his dish. Jeff briefly sniffed the kibble, turned up his nose and walked away.

Kicking off her shoes, Minnie sat down at her desk and opened her laptop. She was up to date on Cassandra's murder. In fact, she probably knew more than or as much as the cops did about it.

Being a stripper gave one much more access to inside information than other people.

Most of her best and loyal customers were cops, lawyers, and private investigators by design. Not only did they trust her, but they assumed she was drunk or high and tended to be quite loose-lipped in their discussions with her. Stereotypes came in handy sometimes.

But it wasn't Cassandra she was interested in just this moment.

It was Frank.

Chapter Three

The unmarked vehicle outside Frank's apartment was one of two things: Tyler, checking up on his old partner and being a normal person, or Tyler and his new partner on a stakeout, seeing if there were going to be more dead strippers appearing thanks to Frank.

I'm on their radar because of The Incident. Because I'm a former cop with a mean streak and a couple of things in my past no one can figure out, Frank thought.

He sat in the dark, near the window, swigging warm beer.

"I'm a likely suspect," Frank said out loud. He rarely talked when he was home. No one to talk to. Even the television, rarely turned on, offered anything concrete to chat about.

He didn't read, not even the newspaper. No computer in the apartment. He wasn't lying to Tyler about losing his phone, either. Frank wasn't interested in being in constant communication with the rest of the world, which could care less about him. It was better this way. He'd eat a meal a day. Maybe two. Spend the rest of his money on cheap beer for home. Get his companionship at the strip club or the occasional hooker.

Life was simple. Wake. Drink. Eat. Strip club. Drink. Sleep. Repeat.

Frank tapped on the glass, looking down at the street and the vehicle. "Now this. Tyler, you know better than to think I had anything to do with this murder."

Of course, if their places had been reversed, Frank would've sought out his former partner as a likely suspect. He'd do everything to clear him as soon as possible or arrest him. Get past it either way and look for the real suspect or have his man in the bag.

Definitely would've been sitting in the car down there, Frank thought.

He went to the kitchen, making sure the lights stayed off. Making it harder for Tyler and his new partner to look into the apartment, although he knew they probably had fancy infrared binoculars and recording devices.

Frank made a pot of coffee. While it was brewing he glanced out the window again to make sure the car was still there.

In the old days it was always Frank's job to make sure the coffee was hot. Tyler brought the donuts or bagels. Frank couldn't remember how many stakeouts they'd been on over the years. All of them were boring. Most of them are worthless, too. Unlike in TV shows, the bad guy doesn't suddenly walk out of his apartment, collar up and shady eyes searching the street, hands in pockets, and head down the sidewalk to be easily followed.

Most of the time the perp is long gone. He's already either in Tacoma visiting a third cousin no one knows about or he's dead. Sometimes they'll stay in their apartment for weeks at a time, ordering Chinese food and their drug dealers swinging by to deliver whatever they need.

In this day and age, a person didn't have to leave their sanctuary. They definitely never wandered aimlessly down a sidewalk if they thought there was heat on them.

Frank poured two cups of coffee in two of his less-chipped coffee cups. He always took his coffee black, but Tyler hated the coffee taste. He preferred light and sweet, the opposite of his women, as he loved to say.

Just like old times, Frank thought. *Me, nearly drunk, getting the coffee so I can be an awake nearly-drunk, and Tyler his usual peppy self. Especially with strong coffee.*

His downstairs neighbor in 1B was playing her awful salsa music again. At least it was lower than it usually was. Frank had stopped opening his window at night because she'd have it on, droning in what had to be an endless song, until morning. It might help her sleep but it kept Frank awake.

He'd seen her once and he liked what he saw: dark-skinned Latina. Curvy. Thick. Loved to wear tight dresses that accented her apple bottom backside and generous pair upfront.

Frank was trying to remember what her name was as he stepped onto the sidewalk and looked around, just like every perp in every TV show did.

There were definitely two silhouettes in the vehicle. Tyler had brought his partner with him, the new kid. This meant they were here on business. To watch Frank. See if he tossed a dead chick from his window or they heard screams as he tortured a stripper.

No one would hear screams over the damn salsa music.

As he approached the headlights came on and Frank stopped in the middle of the street.

Frank grinned and held up the two cups of coffee. "Don't be like that. Where are you going? I brought us coffee." Frank sighed. The nice thing would be to give the new guy the second cup. He wasn't really interested in drinking coffee this late at night, anyway. He'd be up until morning. Too much thinking. Too long to get settled and to sleep with the caffeine running in his veins.

The vehicle started but didn't move away from the curb.

Frank figured Tyler was going to play Super Cop in front of his new partner and they'd go for a ride. A pleasant conversation. See if Frank said anything stupid or lied about anything.

I got nothing to hide, Frank thought. *Just a drunk who likes to be around strippers. That's not a crime. Not yet.*

The driver's window came down just as Frank got to it. It wasn't Tyler.

The guy looked mean. Thick neck. A scar running down the side of his face, which Frank could see even in this poor lighting. In the daytime it would be the guy's most prominent feature. Angry and red.

"Hey," Frank said, thinking about throwing both cups of hot coffee in the guy's face and running.

The Walther PPK aimed at his face said otherwise.

"Is that the new one?" Frank asked. He tried to keep his hands from shaking and spilling coffee. At this range, the weapon would really ruin your day.

The passenger door opened and another man who looked like he'd been hired from Thug Central Casting stepped out. He held a matching Walther PPK.

Frank was going to ask if they were standard issue for whatever criminal syndicate they both worked for. He decided to keep quiet.

"Dump the coffee," the driver said. "And get in the back. Our boss wants to have a chat."

Chapter Four

As Minnie perused the internet looking for information on the cop turned strip club regular, she marveled at the wealth of restricted data she was able to access. When Minnie first moved to Vegas, she was fortunate enough to have met a homicide detective on one of the very first nights she stripped there. He turned out to be quite smitten with her and ended up being a very valuable source of information. Unbenownst to him she had acquired his credentials in order to access his vast database of confidential information. Thankfully, this poor sap was married, which allowed her to keep him on the hook, but quiet about it as well. She had access not only to his database, but also his thoughts on current cases. Minnie loved her damned job.

She had always been fascinated by murder. While other kids were reading Beatrix Potter, Minnie spent her time immersed in the lives of Ted Bundy, Jeffrey Dahmer, and of course the mystery of Jack the Ripper. The *why* interested her the most. What caused someone to want to take a human life? The answer was never clear of course. There were usually a number of factors that led someone to murder. A lethal combination of genetics, brain chemistry, and trauma. But not always. There were some, although rare, who had normal physiology and a lovely childhood who still grew up to be killers. Minnie thought it was nice to be included in this group.

The idea of killing people herself started to creep into her mind as she read about one of the most notorious female serial killers of all time, Aileen Wuornos. She was a street hooker who was as likely to kill her clients as she was to suck their dicks. When she was caught, she said she had killed in self defense. These guys were going to rape and murder her or someone else, although when all was said and done most if not all the men she murdered seemed unlikely to do either. Minnie was not so much a fan of Aileen, as she was intrigued by her.

Minnie considered Aileen to be sloppy, impulsive, and driven by emotion, which is of course why she got caught. She on the other hand was calculating, precise, and always made sure her victims were deserving of her wrath. She considered herself a public servant. Minnie's victims had victims of their own, she was simply dispensing justice. Like a slutty albeit clandestine super hero.

Minnie committed her first act of justice shortly after her 13th birthday. She had been sitting on a park bench with her nose in a book, when one of her peers caught her eye. A girl named Alicia was walking along the concrete edge of the playground holding something close to her chest. Minnie knew Alicia from school, pretty and popular, she always attracted a lot of attention from other kids and teachers alike. On this day, she appeared to not want to be seen. Other than a few moms with strollers and yelping toddlers, the park was pretty much empty. Minnie watched as Alicia slipped unnoticed into the small grove of trees behind the swing set and off the concrete path. She set her bookmark, placed her book in her backpack, and started to follow the other teen.

Keeping a good distance, she was able to see that Alicia held a hamster in her hands. She stood horrified as she watched the popular girl from school hold up the small and unsuspecting rodent close to her face, tiny head in one hand and fat little body in the other, and with one quick motion, twist. The poor creature made no sound as its neck was broken. Minnie was stunned in place as she watched the girl continue to twist the little head like a sick parody of the demon possessed child in *The Exorcist*. She gave one hard yank, and the furry little creature's head separated from its body. No longer interested, Alicia threw the head and body in separate directions, and turned to see Minnie standing there.

Terrified, Minnie started to back away as Alicia said "Hey loser, don't bother telling anyone, you know they won't believe you."

And Minnie knew she was right. In school, Minnie was considered bright, but forgettable. She lacked the middle school clout that came with Alicia's porcelain skin, golden hair, and saccharin laced personality. Minnie left the park without saying a word, and rode her bike back home.

Later in the evening, after dinner, she told her parents she had some work to do and bid them an early goodnight. Minnie did indeed have some work to do. She knew from her studies that killing small animals would be just the beginning. Who would Alicia grow up to kill: her husband, her kids, her parents? Certainly it wouldn't end with a hamster, unless someone was to intervene.

Peanuts were not allowed in her classroom due to some kids' severe even deadly allergies to them. As she loved her PB&J's, Minnie found this an annoyance but accepted it as necessary. Alicia happened to be very vocal about her allergy as a means to much sympathy and attention. She spent the next few days carefully documenting Alicia's routine. She almost always walked with her BFF home from school, except on Tuesdays when her friend attended her music lesson.

The next Tuesday, Minnie delivered a carefully forged note to her last period teacher giving her permission to leave class 30 minutes early. She hurried down the route to Alicia's home and waited. Alicia appeared right on time, spotting Minnie standing under a large tree next to the sidewalk.

Alicia glared at her. "What the fuck are you doing here, loser?"

Minnie said nothing, but held a piece of folded binder paper in the air and started toward a dense patch of vegetation between two empty houses. Alicia, assuming that Minnie had some scrap of embarrassing middle school info followed behind. As she approached, Minnie stepped forward with her index finger extended and suddenly stuck it up the other girl's nostril. Caught completely off guard, Alicia's scream was cut short, as her tissues began to swell. Her hand went from her assaulted nose to her throat as she gasped for breath. Minnie watched with amazement as her face first turned white, then an unnatural shade of blue, and finally a pretty purple that just happened to coordinate with the now dead girl's blouse.

Minnie used a tissue from the package she kept with her for her own seasonal pollen allergies to wipe the smeared blood and peanut butter from her finger. She whistled all the way home.

Her parents told her of the unexpected and somewhat odd tragedy the next morning and asked if she would like to stay home, and she declined the offer. Everyone was sad, crying, and Minnie did her best to join the din. Alicia would have been flattered. Minnie was proud of her accomplishment, but as she ran over it in her mind she realized that she had taken quite a large risk. Without knowing exactly how severe Alicia's allergy actually was, especially given her propensity toward dramatics, her little plot could've easily gone sideways. What would she have done if the anaphylaxis reaction had only been mild? Would she have had to strangle her? Minnie no longer took such risks, and information was key.

As her thoughts returned from mini-Minnie back to the task at hand, her probing led her to an unexpected revelation. Frank, it seemed, had not retired willingly. The depressed regular she mostly just paid lip service to, had an interesting past. She doubted he was involved in Sass's murder however, but she understood now why the two cops had paid him a visit. She also now had reason to suspect they wouldn't be the only ones who might want to have a chat with the ex-cop.

Chapter Five

"Dead strippers are bad for business."

The older guy with the slicked-back hair and sharkskin suit, looking like an extra from *Goodfellas*, was smiling at Frank, toothpick rolling on his lips.

"I'm confused… are you trying to be DeNiro, Pesci or Pacino with your bad accent and cheesy outfit?" Frank took the punch in the gut by the goon on the right with a smile. He dropped down to one knee and tried to catch his breath.

"You're a funny guy." The guy knelt down near Frank, the toothpick threatening to jab him in the eye. "I've heard a lot of things about you, Michi. A couple of them are even flattering." He laughed at his own joke. "A shamed cop. Maybe on the take. Definitely one who cut corners, which is why your past is so soiled."

"What's this about?" Frank asked, staggering back to his feet. The punch had been harder than he'd thought. He wasn't as young as he'd used to be when he'd been roughed up on the streets. Hadn't taken a punch to the gut in years.

He forced back the bile and tried to keep from passing out. "You can't really blame me for a dead stripper."

The guy shook his head. He pulled the toothpick from his mouth, stared at it for a second, and reinserted it. "It's bad for business."

"You said that already." Frank waited for the next punch but so far so good. "How can I help you?"

"What makes you think you can help me?"

Frank shrugged. "If you thought I had anything to do with K.C.'s murder I'd be six feet under by now. Am I right?"

The guy nodded.

"I knew her. I'm a regular in the club. I know most of the dancers, especially the ones who've been around awhile. There are always new girls coming and going for various reasons."

The guy frowned. "What reasons?"

"Bad shifts. Bad customers. The money isn't as good as in another club in town or in another city. Maybe they're only living here for a short time, with a boyfriend or husband who has a new job. A bunch of reasons." Frank grinned, knowing he was about to get punched again. "A lot of times it's because the owner of the place is cheap or sleazy. Usually both."

The guy's head move was subtle.

Frank got punched by the goon on his left. He hit harder, knocking the wind out of Frank and the grin off his face as he dropped to both knees on the cement floor.

"I own this place," the guy said, once again in Frank's face. The toothpick was gone. Frank hoped it wasn't embedded in his forehead. The guy was pissed. "I'm the boss around here. My girls getting killed is bad for business. So are nosy cops hanging around asking too many questions."

Frank wanted to speak, say something snappy, but he couldn't form words. He stayed on his knees and closed his eyes until the room stopped spinning.

"I want you to work for me. Find out who's doing this. It needs to stop, and it needs to go away quietly. Do you understand?"

Frank nodded his head slowly.

"You need to report back to me every other day, unless you find out something important."

Frank opened his eyes and tried to stand. The two goons helped him up, which he thought was nice of them. They'd driven him to his knees, after all.

"What's in it for me? I don't work for free," Frank said.

The guy smiled. "You're in no position to negotiate."

Frank shrugged. "Then beat me up and put me in the hospital or morgue, buddy. I don't give two shits who you are. I have a job. It's keeping my nose out of trouble. Getting wrapped up with someone like you is a bad idea, and I've already made enough bad decisions in my life for six men."

"Do you know who I am?" The guy looked furious. He had a toothpick in his mouth again. Frank wondered if it was the same one or he had a stash in a pocket.

"I don't know and I don't care," Frank said. "The Vegas mob is run back east, so you work for The Family from New Jersey or The Machine in New York. Am I close?"

The guy was furious. "I work for myself. I control several clubs in town. Legitimate businesses, too. Apartment buildings."

"Let me guess… you're my scumbag landlord that won't fix the plumbing?"

The guy smiled, his demeanor changed.

Frank knew this guy was going to be dangerous to deal with, and knew he hadn't been asked to throw in with them and find a killer. He'd been *told*.

"You can call me Mister Santonelli. Friends call me Gus."

Frank sighed. "As in Gus the Animal?"

Both goons stiffened next to Frank, who knew he'd said the wrong thing.

Santonelli shook his head. "You definitely have a huge pair, Michi. I'll give you that. No one calls me that to my face."

Frank shrugged. "I'd be proud of a nickname like that. When I was in elementary school the kids called me Frank the Tank, and not because I was intimidating. It was because I was really fat, and they loved picking on me. Even the girls."

"I'm not an animal," Santonelli said. "I get things done. I follow the rules. I do what needs to be done, whether or not it's pretty. I am a provider for my bosses back east. I stay under the radar in Las Vegas and Reno. I pay off whoever needs to be taken care of. I help the community. I run a legit soup kitchen. A few small businesses that have nothing to do with the others. Strictly moneymakers."

Frank didn't care about the guy's resume but he had no choice but to keep his mouth shut and listen.

"As long as I keep my nose out of trouble and keep sending money back east, no one messes with me. I can do my own thing." Santonelli shook his head. "I never get involved in the day to day operations. You won't see me step into one of my strip clubs or bars. My name isn't on any paperwork. I am strictly the behind the scenes owner."

Frank nodded. "And now this killing has brought the heat. Turned a spotlight on you and your crew. I get it."

"I need the killer or killers found. Brought to me. I will deal with them." Santonelli frowned. "I can't pay off the cops on this one. Too much at stake. I need to add an extra layer, which is you. With your former job and maybe a friend or two on the force, you can be a vital asset."

"What's in it for me?" Frank asked.

"I don't kill you."

Frank shook his head. "I need walking around money. Nothing too much. I don't want anyone getting suspicious. I also need my rent paid and some groceries. I don't think I'm asking for too much."

Santonelli looked like he was thinking about it. "Fine. You won't see me again unless this is solved or you screw me over."

"Sounds fair," Frank said. "Can I go?"

Santonelli shook his head. "After my boys are done letting you know what happens when you openly call me Gus The Animal."

Frank sighed as the two goons began taking turns beating him.

Chapter Six

Dead strippers aren't always bad for business, especially the ones she took out. They were much better for business dead. While rare, the profession itself could be a haven for sociopaths. Minnie wasn't the only homicidal stripper roaming the Vegas strip. Of the dozen or so strippers and prostitutes Minnie had removed from the scene, she was sure at least half were cold blooded killers. The other half being thieves, drug dealers, and under-age sex traffickers. Sass was none of those things.

Sass caught her eye from the moment she stepped on to the stage. Most of the time she only took a passing interest in the new girls who showed up nearly every week. Always a fresh young crop ready to be on their own, most of the new girls realized quickly that this was a rough business. Sass shared the newcomers' naiveté, but Minnie recognized the girl's fortitude and determination. This one had potential, even though Minnie found her wide eyed bubbly personality to be a little irritating at times. While she would never admit it to her face, she liked her, mostly. Minnie would never take a girl under her wing, but would instead keep a close watch on her. Ready to nudge her in the right direction should she need it. Girls like this were rare in Minnie's world. Even though most were good people, not many were strong enough to make it. They fell prey to drugs, alcohol, or bad relationships. Minnie couldn't help these ones, and she didn't really want to. After all, she wasn't Captain Save a Ho. Irritating or not, Sass had potential, and now she was dead.

It was Minnie's job to know people, in both her professional and not-so-professional jobs. While she understood why Frank made a compelling suspect in the murder of a stripper, she was now positive he didn't do it. While it had become apparent that Frank may have some impulse control issues and definitely some ethical issues when it came to his finances, he wasn't a killer. Sass was brutalized in a manner not consistent with Frank's personal faults. She had been beaten so badly that her dental records were rendered useless for the purpose of identification. Lacking any nearby next of kin, Sass was ultimately identified by the serial numbers on her breast implants. Frank wasn't capable of such a thing.

Sass had been at the club for well over a year, a long time for any girl to stay at one club. Vegas had so many clubs, hopping from club to club was common. Due to her wholesome and approachable appearance, she developed a very respectable and lucrative client base. Most of her customers were local and loyal. Lawyers, medical professionals, and business owners were attracted to her wit as well as her looks. She didn't seem to attract the kind of guy who might beat her face in. Minnie checked them out anyways and expectedly came up empty.

Having for the most part, ruled out customers she considered the manager and other staff. The manager, a man with an endless supply of multicolored velour jumpsuits who frequently bought the newbies drinks and got his free "quality control" lap dances. A stereotypical strip club manager with his ever growing bald spot and greasy smile who on special occasions donned a sport coat looked to be made from a dissected faux leather sofa, Steve was the face of the Pink Pussycat.

Minnie knew the owners were from an organization from back east. Steve was disgusting, but also not a killer, and definitely not someone who possessed either the balls or the anger to murder someone. He was content in his sliminess and wouldn't dare mess up the arrangement he had. The bouncers and DJ's also had no motives to murder the girls, they were trying to fuck them not kill them. The owners had an aversion to anything that would bring the wrong kind of attention to the club, and so were also ruled out. They were mean sons of bitches and while they had no qualms about killing, unlike Minnie they considered any dead strippers as a hindrance to business.

So who would want Sass dead? Minnie considered the other dancers. Sass had her haters, but those were common. A pretty girl who comes up quick and makes a lot of money was destined to piss off the other strippers. Petty jealousy was an accepted part of the job. The best bet is to smile in their faces and walk away and wait for the next new girl to attract their attention. Minnie never engaged in such envy or pettiness, she kept her eye on her true purpose. There was one of Sass' haters that Minnie thought had held on a little too long. A woman not a girl who had been on Minnie's radar for some time.

She went by the name Unique, and Minnie thought she was anything but. She had had enough facial surgery to erase any and all uniqueness she may have once possessed. Overdone boobs and a questionable butt lift had left her looking more like a blow up doll than an actual woman. She got her fair share of drunken bachelor party guys and spring breakers, but her shine had faded long ago. She had been at this club for well over a decade and was acutely aware her relevance was quickly on the decline. That fact alone made her the prime suspect in this murder.

Minnie had become aware of Unique's attempts at sabotaging other girls' money. Including a particularly vicious incident where she had replaced one poor dancer's body spray with the liquid from a can of tuna. The victim in this case had doused herself, as most dancers do, before noticing the odor. Unique denied responsibility of course, but Minnie knew better.

Unique's attacks on her competition escalated and Minnie knew they would only get worse as her supply of self esteem depleted. Although she had yet to be violent or cause any lasting damage, Minnie knew it was only a matter of time. She now feared she may have waited too long to get rid of this one.

Unique lived in the north part of town, well past the strip and far beyond where tourists dared to tread. Her ever declining income had her in the drug infested and dark park of Vegas only the hardiest of locals knew of. She had a small one bedroom apartment tucked neatly behind a rundown casino that existed because of the junkies and drunks not allowed in the more respectable establishments. She almost felt sorry for the dilapidated stripper, but any genuine sympathy was squashed as she was now convinced Unique had killed Sass. She dressed in all black, tied her hair up, and tucked her favorite buck knife in her waistband and headed out the door.

As she pulled up in the alleyway behind the apartment building of the soon to be dead stripper, Minnie caught a glimpse of something in her rear view mirror. She wondered if she may have been followed. Were the cops looking at Frank also looking at her? Unlikely. She had come a long way from the risky incident with Alicia, but she could make out the dark silhouettes of two men in the front of the vehicle. No matter who they were, it wouldn't be wise to stay where she was. Unique it seemed had been granted a brief reprieve. As she pulled away, the other car stayed put.

As she drove back to her apartment, her mind flashed briefly to the night of Sass' murder. Although she remembered leaving the club well before midnight, her mind's eye saw Sass lying on the pavement broken and bleeding, chest barely moving as she took her last breaths. An almost imperceptible feeling of rage passed through her, and she thought, *stupid bitch had it coming*. The thought frightened her for a split second, and she had to remind herself that she was one of the good guys.

Chapter Seven

Tyler couldn't help but smile when he saw the shape Frank was in: beaten and bloody, with a bag of frozen peas on his forehead and his lip bleeding profusely.

"Who ran you over?" Tyler asked.

"Two goons who think I had something to do with a dead stripper." Frank groaned. "I didn't, by the way. You're barking up the wrong tree as usual. You were never really good with actual police work, buddy."

"Care to tell me who did this? I can protect you." Tyler said it, knowing Frank was going to frown at the comment.

Frank frowned. "Can we not do this dance today? I don't feel so good. I need to go home and take a long bath and a longer nap."

Tyler shook his head. "I'm doing this as a courtesy." he glanced at his new partner, J.C., seated at the counter of the restaurant and staring at a menu like he'd never seen one before. "If I bring the kid over, this becomes official. You get it?"

"I'm not that far removed from being on that side of the table," Frank said. He took a sip of his coffee. "You buying me breakfast?"

"I thought you needed a bath and a nap?"

Frank shrugged. "I can do them both on a full stomach." He sighed. "What do you know about The Family? Asking for a friend."

Tyler shook his head. "You're in too deep as usual. Let me pull you out of this, Frank. I can protect you."

"Nope." Frank waved at the waitress as she approached. "French toast. Side of bacon. Side of scrambled eggs. Side of hash browns. Side of sausage. Whatever he's having."

Tyler waved her off, glancing at his untouched cup of coffee. "You're making a mistake, as usual."

"You made the mistake by not putting someone on me last night," Frank said. "I figured it was you and your new boyfriend there, sitting in the car. I even brought you coffee."

Tyler grinned. "You do still care about me."

"Go to Hell. I had a long night. I don't need protection, but someone asked me to look into her death, and it was more telling than asking, if you know what I mean."

"You need to stay out of this." Tyler caught J.C. staring at him and knew he'd get antsy sooner than later. He hadn't been around long enough to know patience won out over everything else when it came to police work in this town, where every three out of four people were from somewhere else. "This isn't a social visit. For whatever reason, people still think you were a good cop and a good guy. They hate seeing you like this."

"Like what?"

Tyler sighed. "I don't know… sitting in a diner at six in the morning with a bag of peas on your head? That doesn't give off the illusion you're successful."

"Granted, I have had better days." Frank smiled at the waitress and tapped his empty coffee cup. "This isn't mob related, I can tell you that. I'm not even sure it's personal. My gut tells me we're going to see an uptick in dancers getting taken out. How many have there been in the last twelve months?"

"I'm not sharing info with you, Frank. Please, I'm begging you… walk away. Let the cops do their job. You're not part of this anymore. You got out."

"More like I was driven out."

Tyler knew Frank would argue the point to death. It was one of his character flaws and strengths. "Be that as it may… as a friend, I'm asking you to let me do my job and don't get in the way."

"Am I a suspect?"

Tyler shrugged. "A person of interest. I'd like to clear you but I know you're not going to steer clear of this mess."

"I'm not," Frank said. "It's piqued my interest… and when a mobster asks you to look into it, well…" Frank shrugged and thanked the waitress as she started putting heaping plates of food in front of him.

"Walk away, Frank." Tyler stood. He took out his wallet and dropped a twenty on the table. "The change is for the tip."

"I don't want your pennies," Frank said. "You were always a lousy tipper, too."

Tyler leaned close to Frank, making sure not to get too close. Between the smell and the bruises, it wasn't pretty. "As I said… this is a courtesy. If you get in the way I'll be forced to take you down."

"Last time I checked, this was a free country. Thanks for breakfast, Tyler. I'll be seeing you around." Frank put his bag of peas down on the table and began eating like there was no tomorrow.

Tyler walked away, motioning for his partner to follow.

"What was that all about?" J.C. asked as soon as they got outside.

"That was what you do for an old partner and former cop," Tyler said, an edge to his voice. He didn't have time to explain everything to this kid, and he didn't want to. No one had talked him through his miscues. He was expected to show the guy the ropes and nothing more. It wasn't like they were friends. He'd be another young kid who'd eventually decide being a cop in Vegas wasn't as lucrative as being a pit boss, bouncer or gambler.

"We need to go see our tech crew. Find out all we can on The Family," Tyler said. He could see by the look on J.C.'s face he had no idea who The Family was. "New Jersey mobsters. Sounds like they're headed west, or at least looking in our direction. We need to see how far their hooks are in the scene and if it has anything to do with dead strippers."

J.C. shrugged and got in the unmarked car.

Tyler was glad he didn't ask any more questions, because he didn't have any answers to give the guy. Frank was always an unknown commodity, even back in the day when they patrolled together.

He'd been on the take, and he'd gotten busted for it. Tyler's hands hadn't exactly been clean, but he'd wisely stayed away from Frank's shady business dealings.

"You don't think Frank Michi is our killer," J.C. said. "Neither do I."

"It isn't about what we think, kid. It's about what the evidence tells us. We need to figure this out before another pretty girl is found with her throat slashed open," Tyler said.

Frank, please don't get in the way, Tyler thought. *You're not going to like what I'll be forced to do.*

Chapter Eight

She slept, sort of. Her dreams were a disjointed mess of blood, silent screams, and fake eyelashes. As she flirted with slumber and half wakefulness, Minnie tossed and turned in a tangled bundle of sweat dampened sheets and blankets. She finally awoke for good late in the morning with Jeff resting heavily on her chest. *Stupid fucking cat,* she thought as she rolled to the side of the bed forcing the feline to shift off her and on to the floor. He started toward her bedroom door stopping every few feet to look at her, confirming she was going to follow him to the kitchen. Which she did, of course. When she got there she filled his dish with kibble, but also opened a can of the foul smelling wet food he liked, hoping it would keep him from giving her the death stare for an hour or two. She admired his ability to bend her will to his every whim. God, how she loved this insufferable beast.

As the coffee machine began to create its glorious black liquid, the nightmares began to fade from her awareness. She was used to sleeping poorly, but lately the dreams had become more intense. They left her feeling unsettled, even as the details remained murky. Her thoughts morphed from her nightmares to her failed attempt to rid Sin City of its latest malignant stripper. Who the fuck was in that car behind her last night? Did they even have anything to do with her, Unique, or Sass' murder? In the daylight, the notion now seemed paranoid. She was a brilliant killer, her confidence confirmed by the fact that she had never been a suspect or even just a person of interest in any of her previous exploits. Not even her first one, as unsophisticated as it had been. No way was she going soft now. Unique would die today.

She planned on working tonight. She knew it was also Unique's regular shift. With Sass' death so recent, she didn't dare take her out at the club. She would have to get her before sunset. Sipping her coffee Minnie contemplated her options. She had been watching Unique for a while now and was familiar with her habits. It was Friday, which meant she may be meeting one of her outcall clients before work.

Unique sometimes met certain gentlemen at one of the smaller casinos in town, not the high end spots preferred by the pricier hookers. Unique was well past her prime and had to take what she could get. Friday afternoons were an opportune time for a discreet quickie at a seedy hotel with a married businessman on his lunch break. Minnie had to get moving if she were to catch her there.

Not bothering to shower, she threw on a pair of baggy jeans, sweatshirt, and threw her hair in a careless ponytail ensuring she would not elicit any catcalls. She would fit right in with the opioid induced zombies in the part of town she was heading to. She decided her bike would be the best mode of transportation at this hour, and headed off to hopefully find her prey with the taste of an unhappily married man's dick still on her tongue.

She arrived at Unique's preferred rendezvous spot and was delighted to see her cliché red Mustang parked at the hotel. She was even more pleased to find she had parked in a desolate spot near the back of the building. She scanned the outside of the structure for cameras.

In person security was unlikely given the fact that the owner of this establishment likely gave no fucks about security, and found there were none. She took a moment to take some deep breaths as the excitement of the hunt quickened her heartbeat. She was going to enjoy this, a little too much maybe? *No fuck that*, she thought, *she was doing Vegas and the world in fact, a favor.* Her heart was still beating rapidly as she saw her target come out of the door used by the hotel service workers.

Unique didn't hear Minnie padding behind her in her soft soled running shoes, nor did she feel her breath on the back of her neck as she quickly threw the garrote around her throat and pulled it taut. Minnie took in long luxurious breaths of air as she strangled the troublesome old stripper, mostly to spite her, but partly to control her adrenaline rush. She couldn't see her face, but as she felt the life ebb out of her, Minnie welcomed the heat in her crotch. She held on long after the woman was dead before finally letting her fall to the ground with a satisfying thud. Minnie gave herself a mental pat on the back for avenging the death of an annoying but otherwise innocent colleague.

Minnie glanced around to make sure she was still alone and unseen, then secreted the garrote back in her sweatshirt front pocket. She hopped on her bike and headed back home, tossing the handmade murder weapon in a dumpster on her way making sure to wipe it clean of fingerprints. Although Minnie had never been in any kind of trouble, her fingerprints were on file. The city of Las Vegas required strippers to undergo background checks and fingerprints to obtain the proper licensing.

She hoped that for her next victim, she would be able to prepare a more creative demise. Strangulation was perhaps her least favorite method of dispatching unwanted vermin. She liked them to feel it; she wanted them to know they were being removed from this world for their transgressions. This way was far too gentle, but in this case it was necessary to move as quickly as possible. She was still unsure if someone was getting close to her so speed and extra caution was prudent. She made a promise to herself to savor the experience next time.

Jeff welcomed her with what looked like an approving expression, if cats are capable of such a look, as she opened the door to her apartment. Minnie suddenly realized she was ravenously hungry. She cooked up a quick meal of chicken, brown rice, and veggies. As she ate, she recounted the events that just took place. Reveling in the contentment she felt after yet another successful mission. She doubted if anyone would even notice Unique missing her shift tonight, one of the reasons flaky strippers made such convenient victims. Minnie shared a few regulars with the dead stripper, but she would now happily take on the extra work and money. An added perk to her clandestine duties of justice. Minnie, as Venus, would make sure Unique's customers would quickly forget all about her. The police would likely look to her client at the hotel, the poor guy, when they found her body.

With a full stomach, she stripped and laid down naked on her bed, not bothering to pull back the covers, and fell almost instantly into a beautifully deep sleep. She did not dream.

Chapter Nine

Old cop habits were hard to break, even after a long layoff. Frank knew something was wrong tonight. He just needed to figure out what it was. He knew it undoubtedly had to do with another dead stripper.

The likelihood of Unique drunk or drugged out somewhere instead of dead was about even odds to Frank, but his gut told him she was a goner. Another victim.

He'd gotten a bit tipsy tonight, and he knew he should've stayed home. He had his old partner and his old partner's new partner watching his every move. The mobsters asking him for favors. Who knew who else was staring at him, even now, as he smiled at Venus onstage.

She was cute. Intense. When she wasn't looking, Frank would stare at her. Not in lust, although he'd love to see how those tits really felt and if she enjoyed a bit of ass play, but when she thought no one was noticing her. Those few brief moments each night when all eyes were somewhere else.

Venus was the kind of woman that knew what she was doing. She made her money, got a guy off just enough so he'd come back for more, and kept her nose clean. He'd never heard whispers about her getting into trouble with pills and alcohol. Frank knew, if he checked with Tyler, she'd have a clean sheet. This pretty lady was all about the money.

"Another beer?" Cinnamon asked, trying to stifle a yawn.

Frank smiled. "Tell me something… is it often Unique calls out?"

Cinnamon frowned. "How do you know about her no show?"

"I heard a couple of the dancers talking."

Cinnamon shrugged. "It's not the first time, although she's been good in the last couple of months. Ever since Steve took her off the floor and went up one side and down the other. I'm guessing he'll fire her now."

"Seems odd she'd take a chance," Frank said. He took a sip of his beer. "Anyone else call out or acting weird?"

"She didn't call out. No show… but you knew that already." Cinnamon smiled. "Am I a suspect, detective?'

"I'm not a detective and I'm just making small talk. Old habits are hard to break."

Cinnamon leaned over the bar and Frank tried not to lose himself in her cleavage. "You think Unique was murdered?"

Frank shrugged. He didn't want to get anyone excited and definitely not one of the other strippers, although if they were wary it might keep them safe. "I wouldn't be alone if you can help it. Might not be safe. Any of these sleazy bastards could be a killer."

"Sleazy comes with the territory, especially in a town like this. Scumbags come and go all the time. The only thing we have to our advantage is the fact most of them are here for a long weekend, act like an asshole, and then go back to their shitty lives somewhere else." Cinnamon smiled faintly. "I'm worried about Unique. She was into some bad things."

"Like what?"

A loud customer started yelling at Cinnamon for a drink and she wandered over, leaving Frank to his beer and thoughts.

Mike the DJ was drunk and telling the crowd Krystal with a K was coming to the stage, a dancer Frank wasn't too familiar with. He'd seen her only a couple of times and she had some moves. She was what his mama would've called bottom heavy, and he was fine with that. Junk in the trunk was very attractive to him. He might even give up one of his dollars if she came over.

Frank took a look at Mike in the booth and frowned. He was leaning over the rail, headphones dangling, arguing with a guy in a suit. And not a cheap suit, either.

This guy was muscle for the owner, or someone from the outside not supposed to be inside. Frank would need to keep an eye on him. See if he was passing through or going to stay.

If he worked for Santonelli... Frank shook his head. Gus Santonelli had made it perfectly clear it was Frank's problem with dead strippers. He'd steer clear and watch from a discreet distance. If Frank figured out who the killer was and passed it along to Santonelli, Frank had no doubt the guy responsible would be buried in pieces in the desert. If the killer wasn't ever found, Frank made for a good scapegoat when Santonelli was pissed about it.

Frank made a mental note of the dancers working tonight. He'd need to stop drinking and go home and take some actual notes, too. He had no idea how many clubs and dancers for those clubs there were in Vegas, and how many women stayed for long and how many were just passing through. Hundreds of potential targets? Was it tied to this specific club, or based on the dancer herself? K.C. Sass and

Unique had nothing in common look-wise. Other than tight bodies and a shared profession.

In the good old days, creeps would kill a few hookers who reminded them of their moms, Frank mused. They'd steer clear of the strippers because the Mob controlled not only the casinos but the clubs, too. All part of the structure of Las Vegas. It all worked. A nice balance, too.

Now, with organized crime mostly run out of town, it was the Wild West in the desert.

There wasn't enough protection and not nearly enough enforcers to make sure something like this didn't happen. The police were overworked with crimes the Mob used to take care of. Again… it worked.

A guy wearing too-tight jeans, a pink t-shirt and an Oakland Raiders ball cap caught Frank's eye because he'd been watching him for awhile.

When Frank realized who it was he shook his head and stared directly back until the guy got up and headed for the door.

Frank cut him off with a smile. "Officer. Can I help you with something?"

"Get out of my way," J.C. Forrestt said to Frank.

"You look weird not wearing the rookie cop undercover outfit," Frank said. "Did Tyler send you to spy on me?"

"No." J.C. was looking past Frank, who turned to see what he was looking at.

Frank smiled. "Ahh. I see you're admiring Venus. She is quite the pretty gal. Great ass, too. She'll gladly take your money but watch out… I hear she bites."

"Go to Hell." J.C. pushed past Frank and stepped outside. He got a few feet and stopped to light a cigarette just as Frank came outside.

The air felt good after sitting inside for hours. Frank took in a deep breath. "You from L.A.?"

J.C. nodded but didn't look at Frank.

"This was a pleasure outing. You weren't watching me. You were watching Venus," Frank said.

J.C. didn't respond. He took another drag of his cigarette.

"I guess you already know another dancer might be missing," Frank said.

J.C. turned to look at Frank but didn't say anything.

Frank shrugged. "I hate doing your job, but… you might want to check on a dancer. Goes by the name of Unique. She's a no show tonight."

J.C. tossed his cigarette into the street and walked away.

Chapter Ten

Venus was on fire tonight. Renewed from the afternoon's activities and some much needed rest, she was killing it. On stage, in VIP, she was in full red hot goddess mode and her tiny clutch purse was becoming hard to close. She caught that ex-cop Frank staring at her when he thought she wasn't looking. She was always looking, an advantage of being sober. The side eye he was giving her gave her the impression he was wondering what her tits felt like. *Fucking awesome, Frank, absolutely awesome,* she thought. Not that he'd ever find out. Those dances were well beyond his budget.

As her stage finished, one of the bouncers swept her dollars into a pile and into the plastic basket kept for such purposes. She took it to the manager's office so she could change them into bigger bills. As much as she loved her job, she absolutely hated one dollar bills. Nothing irritated her quite like guys making it rain. What a mess and a pain in the ass. Not only did she have to stop what she was doing to wait for one of the meatheads to sweep it up, but the manager took 10% when she traded them in, on top of all the other fees and tips they took. Greedy fucking bastard Steve did it extra slow for her too. It wasn't that he was really into her, his type was much more the typical blonde bimbo stripper, but that he knew she didn't like him. Of course she played it sweet and nice for him, but her contempt was impossible to hide.

Trying to stuff the twenties and hundreds into her purse was pointless, so she walked toward the dressing room to stash the cash into her locker. As she pushed open the door, the familiar aroma of cheap body spray and sushi farts assaulted her nose. One of the girls was offering advice to another: "Lick his balls after you lick his ass to get the taste out of your mouth."

Cute, she thought to herself. As she listened, the context became a little more clear, the girl was speaking about her boyfriend and not a client. Minnie was mildly relieved. She started turning the dial on her lock and heard another, far more interesting conversation taking place.

"Unique was supposed to bring me a bag tonight, stupid bitch, probably kept it for herself and got too high to come to work," said a dark haired girl who called herself Brooklyn.

Minnie turned the dial a little more slowly. Listening more intently.

"Nah," said another girl, a blonde who went by Lexus.

Minnie must have known at least a hundred Lexuses, more than a few Mercedes, and even a Caprice. An unfortunate choice in that instance, because that poor girl had an ass the size of a Chevy.

"She's been clean, and she's been hanging around a guy she really likes. She says he's going to leave his wife. I bet she's with him," Lexus said. "I bet she'll have your stuff when she comes in next. Did you text her?"

"Yeah, bitch went dark," Brooklyn replied. "Haven't heard from her since yesterday. She was only clean for a week or two. She's high somewhere."

Minnie opened her locker and put her money in her backpack. She took a long drink of her bottled water, grabbed a piece of gum and doused herself with her own cheap body spray to mask the smell of stale cigarette smoke.

"After what happened to Cass, I really hope she's ok," Lexus whined. "She was so nice."

What the fuck? Minnie thought. Unique was a cunt of the highest order. Sometimes these girls were too dumb to see when people were taking advantage of them. Deluded and taken in by Unique's facade of the helpful experienced dancer, trying to teach the new generation. Probably not even suspecting Unique was a cruel saboteur out to undermine them while smiling in their faces. They'll probably be all upset when they find out she's dead. Light some candles and all that shit. The blissful ignorant, doomed to live in the dark. Good thing someone was protecting them.

Minnie became Venus as she left the dressing room and stepped back on to the floor. She stood by the bar as she scanned the room for her next mark. She saw Frank step in front of a guy as he was headed out the door. The guy had on an ensemble she thought was the dorkiest outfit she had ever seen. So dorky in fact, that she concluded he must be a cop. Trying and failing to not look like a cop, and she recognized him as one of the cops that had been talking to Frank. She smiled at him when he looked over at her. She was having a hard time discerning whether he was here for business or pleasure. She didn't think Unique had been found yet. A creepy little tendril of dread started to wind itself into her brain. Two dead strippers from the same club would likely draw attention. She couldn't help but wonder if she had committed a fatal error, but quickly dismissed the thought. They had been killed by totally different methods and in different locations. Not to mention, she had only killed one of them, the bad one.

Cinnamon came up behind her. "Unique didn't make it in tonight, I heard someone say she was murdered."

Venus turned her head and rolled her eyes before replying. "That's ridiculous. Strippers are flaky. I'm sure she's fine. Ooh, there's a nice one, catch you later."

Venus strutted as quickly away on her seven inch platforms toward the nearest nice looking customer. She hadn't really decided on approaching him, but the last thing she wanted to do was get stuck in a conversation with the ever nosy Cinnamon. Trying to pull out of a dialogue with that one was like trying to pull your foot out of a mud puddle without losing your shoe. Cinnamon had a bad habit of running her mouth. Sometimes the things she blurted out could be detrimental to other dancers. A slip of personal information about a girl to a customer could ruin her money, or encourage a stalker. Cinnamon had the very real potential to get one of these girls hurt or killed even. That spicy sweet smile and tone of voice hid carelessness, maybe even malice toward other dancers. Might be a good idea to check that one out sometime.

The customer watched her approach with interest. His eyelids looked like they weighed a ton and he had a goofy smile on his face. As he greeted her, the smell of cheap tequila wafted out of his face. "You come here often?" he slurred, overestimating his own cleverness.

"First time. Maybe you could show me where the VIP room is?" she said, matching his goofy smile.

Chapter Eleven

Tyler smiled when he saw how uncomfortable J.C. was. *Just another dead body*, Tyler thought. *You've seen one... you've seen 'em all.*

It wasn't necessarily true. He'd seen bodies pulled from the water after the skin had stretched to the breaking point, gases finding ways to escape and rip the flesh. Fish had picked the eyes from the corpse, the fingers and toes a delicious meal for bigger predators. The smell once you fished the body out of the water was the worst. Once you had that in your nose you never forgot it, and never got rid of it.

It was Unique, if you used her dancer name. Tyler didn't really care what her real name was. He'd let J.C. take the lead on this one. It shouldn't be too hard to find the DNA of a john inside her and try to see if there were prints on her fake tits.

"Are you going to be sick?" Tyler asked, trying not to openly laugh. A couple of uniformed officers nearby were grinning. They likely had a bet if J.C. was going to puke or not.

Whoever had *he's gonna puke* was the winner.

J.C. walked about twenty feet away and tossed his dinner into a bush. He took a deep breath, shook his head, and went back to stand near Tyler. "I'm fine. Got a piece of bad fish."

That made everyone laugh, but not too loud. They all knew the news would pull up any minute. It would be in poor form to have a bunch of cops standing around a dead body smiling.

"You're the lead on this one, but I'll be watching," Tyler said.

J.C. frowned. "What'd I do wrong?"

"Nothing. It's just time. This should be an easy one, too. Go by the book and hopefully you'll have our killer in handcuffs in a few days." Tyler shrugged. "Unless he's not in the system and he's likely not a local. Which means, by the time everything comes back, we could be looking at some mook from Cleveland who came to town to gamble and get laid, but it took a bad turn."

J.C. nodded. "I got this."

"Good. I'm going for a ride."

J.C. looked confused. "Where? We just got here. This is a crime scene."

"Unless you think I did this and want to arrest me, officer… I need some coffee and a muffin." Tyler leaned in closer to J.C. "And I'll bring you a breath mint from the car. You had a few tonight."

"I was off-duty." J.C. looked away.

"Where?"

"Out with friends."

"Bullshit." Tyler put a hand on his partner's shoulder. "You know I'll find out."

J.C. sighed. "Not that thing. I told you I'm not gonna touch it. Too hot right now. I mean, the money will be great, but…"

"But it's too hot. There are eyes on it right now." Tyler shook his head. "You need to learn patience. If we did that move right now we'd be in trouble. I have a guy in Reno who can move that big a haul, but not yet. Just stop thinking about it. That's your retirement fund, but you're still too young to enjoy it without anyone being suspicious. Now… where were you out drinking?"

J.C. looked away again. "The strip club."

Tyler groaned. "Please tell me you didn't do anything stupid."

"I went to do a follow-up. That's all," J.C. said.

That didn't seem likely to Tyler. He knew the kid was a good cop but he wasn't great. He had no real drive to him. He was by the book when it mattered but took no initiative. J.C. wasn't going to ever be an alpha male lead detective no matter how much experience he got. It was the reason Tyler had pushed so hard to bring him under his wing. He needed a guy who would do what he was told, took whatever portion of a cut Tyler was willing to give him, and do the grunt work. No one was going to get rich off of a cop's salary.

They stood in silence and Tyler knew J.C. was going to break.

He did. "I went for myself. Okay? I hadn't been in a strip club in forever. Since college. I just wanted to relax on my day off. Grab a beer. See some dancing."

"Which one?" Tyler asked.

J.C. frowned. "Which one what?"

"Tell me which dancer you went to see tonight. No bullshit, either. This is important."

"Venus. She's hot."

Tyler laughed. "She's dangerous. They all are. No stripper in their right mind would date one of us. Too much drama for both sides. You want to slip her a twenty for her to grab your little pecker? Knock yourself out. After this case is done. It will look odd if anyone places you there tonight."

"Why?"

Tyler still had his hand on J.C.'s shoulder. Now he gave it a squeeze. "Two dead strippers, both from the same club."

"Maybe. They get around, you know."

Tyler groaned again. He held up two fingers. "Strippers. Dead. Two. Same club you're in again, drooling over a stripper. If she turns up dead next weekend you're royally fucked. You get that? You go nowhere without me. Especially to see tits. Lesson learned?"

J.C. nodded.

"Follow me to the car for a breath mint. You could knock a buzzard off a shit wagon with what's coming out of your pie hole," Tyler said. "Forensics should be here any minute. Then the real work begins."

"Can you get me a coffee and a donut?" J.C. asked.

"That'll look great on the morning news. A cop eating a donut and drinking coffee at a crime scene." Tyler smiled. "I'll get it but we'll keep it all in the car. Act like you forgot your pen or something every now and then and take a hit."

"Hey… about the other thing…"

Tyler sighed. "Not another word about it."

J.C. wisely changed the subject. "Your buddy Frank was also in the club tonight."

"He's a permanent fixture."

"He's an asshole," J.C. said.

Tyler smiled. "That he is… but he's a useful asshole. You'll see."

Chapter Twelve

Minnie awoke to the soft sound of thunder or what her half dreaming mind thought was thunder. The low rumble was coming from Jeff who was perched on her chest. When she opened her eyes she was greeted by the menacing stare of her furry master nestled between her boobs. His cold wet nose almost touching hers, the look in his eyes was either one of unadulterated love or homicidal malice tempered by the fact he lacked the thumbs required to open a can of cat food. Minnie couldn't be sure. Either way, she wasn't going back to sleep until she did his bidding, and probably not after either. She had slept like a corpse.

"Come on fucker," she said as she nudged the small beast off her chest and got out of bed. Not bothering to put anything on, she walked to the kitchen nude. Jeff hurried to get in front of her, stopping every few feet in a nefarious attempt to trip her. As she reached for a can of his favorite unidentified innards of what may or may not have been a chicken, he howled as if he hadn't eaten in days. Although his considerable belly made his insinuations of starving look wildly inaccurate.

The smell of the cat food turned her stomach. The odor wouldn't last long as Jeff was lapping it up as if he was indeed starving. Minnie pushed the button on her coffee maker and soon the stench of Jeff's meal was obliterated altogether.

It was late afternoon, and as she sipped her coffee in her kitchen. Still nude as she rarely wore clothing while at home, her thoughts turned to the night before. Might have been a record breaker. By the time she left the club the sun was up. She felt like a used dish rag, damp and smelling of cigarette smoke, sweat, and the horny desperation of Sin City. She badly needed a shower.

As she rinsed the strip club off her body, she remembered she hadn't even bothered to count her take from the night before. Not only had she had her own regular customers, but had managed to snag a few of Unique's as well. One in particular was quite annoyed that she hadn't shown up for work that night, as he had texted her that he was coming into town. He assumed that Unique had fallen off the wagon and was fucked up somewhere. Minnie didn't have to mention her at all, but managed to take all the cash he had brought with him and had even convinced him to hit the ATM not once, but twice.

Her intention hadn't been to take out the old stripper to steal her customers, but it sure was a nice bonus. If anyone ever thought to suspect her of the killing, not that they would, the added income would seem like a terrific motive. Especially if they didn't bother to see what a piece of trash Unique actually was. As she thought about it now, she wondered if they would find anything to tie Unique to Sass's killing. Minnie wished she would've left something to point them in that direction, but it was over now. They would pin them both on a couple of john's. Another perk of her extracurricular activities, women were almost never suspects.

Wrapped in a bath towel Minnie went to her safe. In her exhaustion, she had simply tossed the cash in the bottom. Now she grabbed it with both hands and sorted the different denominations on the floor. Finally able to count it, she saw it was a record breaking night, maybe even the best she'd ever had. Minnie decided she had earned a few nights off. Shit, she had earned a few weeks off, but a few nights would suffice. She sent a text to the manager letting him know she wouldn't be in for a while. With all the cops sniffing around the club lately, a break seemed like a really good idea. Although she knew that at least one of them may have been using the murders as an excuse to hang out at the club. She thought they may have been investigating tits and ass a little more than the untimely death of a known drug addicted stripper.

Minnie called and made a reservation at her favorite retreat up at Mt Charleston just outside of Vegas. She booked three nights. It was the middle of the week, so it would be empty. This place had full spa services, a heated pool, and a fabulous restaurant. She fully intended to take advantage of it. Jeff would have to come along too, given that Minnie had no one she trusted to take care of him. He wouldn't mind though. He would be content shedding his fur in a luxury suite. Jeff had been traveling with her his whole life, and while he surely wouldn't admit it if he could talk, she thought he actually enjoyed it.

After grabbing a light snack, Minnie packed a bag with only the bare essentials for her and her hairy charge and set out. As the freeway turned into a mountain road, she couldn't help but smile a bit. As soon as she got to her room, she freed Jeff from his carrier, which looked nothing like an animal carrier. Cats or any pets for that matter were strictly forbidden here and most of the places she took him. Including her own apartment. He hopped out and began to eye his temporary accommodations.

Then she turned off her phone. She had no intention of using screens of any type while she was here. She ordered a decadent meal of grilled swordfish, veggies, and her favorite dessert, death by chocolate. She pulled out one of the three books she had brought with her, all part of a zombie series, and started to read as she waited for her food.

Her food was spectacular even though she had to sacrifice a piece of fish to Jeff, who made it clear he would make her sorry if she didn't share. Ignoring her mother's warning about waiting a half hour after eating to swim, she put on her swimsuit and headed down to the pool. She would have preferred to swim naked of course, but sometimes concessions have to be made. The last thing she wanted while on her little vacation was to attract any attention. The water was lovely, and she had closed her eyes in bliss. Mind emptied of murdered strippers, cops, and horny old men; she was caught unaware when a man entered the pool area.

"Why hello there," he said, his voice sounding lewd. Startled, Minnie started to swim to the steps to exit. She did not respond.

"I didn't mean to startle you. What's your name?" He tried again.

Again Minnie stayed silent. One of the reasons she came to this spot was because it was a couples retreat. She had been here at least a dozen times and had only seen a few single people here. This was not a welcome development. Minnie was not pleased. She grabbed her towel and made to leave. The pool area was small and fenced in, and as she neared the gate the man stepped toward her and tried, almost succeeding, to grab her by the arm.

"I was just leaving. I'm not in the mood for company," she said as she deftly avoided his grasp. "Well fuck you, you stuck up bitch!" He spit and looked as if he might reach for her again. She shot him a look that stopped him dead in his tracks. He backed away as if he thought she might hit him. It was his turn to look startled.

When she got back to her room, Jeff was not sleeping as she expected. He was alert and wearing an expression of irritation. The expression of irritation didn't alarm her, as it was pretty much his default look. The fact he wasn't dozing did. Had someone been in her room? She had hung the do not disturb sign on the knob and had let the front desk know that she wouldn't be requiring room service. She never did, but something seemed off. If a staff member had been in her room, they would have likely seen Jeff and thrown a tantrum over him. She inspected the rest of her things and found nothing out of place nor anything missing, but the eerie feeling of violation persisted.

Chapter Thirteen

J.C. knew he was sliding down a slippery slope, but he couldn't stop it.

Is this piece of ass worth my career? Worth getting in trouble over? No woman is, especially a lowlife stripper, he thought. Trying to convince himself to turn his car around and go home. Fantasize about her. Masturbate until he got blisters thinking about her.

This is insane, J.C. thought, staring into her windows. He caught a glimpse of her in the kitchen. He sat up in the seat. Was she naked?

J.C. groaned. She was nude. Walking around her place like it was nothing. The blinds not fully drawn. This was exciting and so wrong, all at the same time. It was one thing to stare at her in the strip club, when she was shaking her amazing ass and tits onstage. To be at her private residence like this…

He was doing police work. He knew he could frame it in his mind so it worked for him as well as anyone who asked. Especially Tyler, who was going to wonder where he was.

With the crime scene from last night buttoned up and the search ongoing for the killer, the only thing left to do was canvas the neighborhood. Which was ridiculous. There was nothing but casinos and tourists coming and going. Anyone who had even thought they'd seen something was likely halfway back to Kansas by now.

J.C. lost sight of her. He slumped back down in his vehicle. He wanted to touch himself. Think about her again. Caught in a car with his dick in his hands, though, was beyond saving his career. No talking your way out of it.

His phone vibrated on the seat next to him. He glanced at it, knowing it was going to be his partner. He stared at the phone but didn't answer it. Tyler would leave a message.

Technically he was on his own for the next few hours, asking questions and keeping busy. He'd tell Tyler he'd gone in and out of the casinos and asked them for surveillance footage, which they wouldn't turn over without a warrant. It would give him time.

Time for what? J.C. groaned again. It wasn't like he could waltz over to her door and knock. Ask if he could come in. Touch those amazing tits and fuck her on the couch.

She'd been staring at him at the club, but it could be because she knew he was staring. Like every other asshole who had a wad of cash in his pocket. Next to his raging hard-on.

Leave. Go back to work. This is wrong, J.C. thought.

He didn't see her moving around anymore. Had she gone back to bed? Strippers slept in. They were night owls. Maybe she got hungry, made a quick bite, and went back to sleep. She might have crashed on the couch. Nude. Vulnerable. Ready for the taking.

What the fuck is wrong with you? Jeez. I'm not that guy. I've never been that guy. She's a fantasy. Out of my league.

Get it together and go home. Whack off again and then get back to work, J.C. thought.

His inner angel and devil fought for control and he gripped the dashboard in desperation. He took a deep breath and put his hand on the key.

Start the car. Drive away.

Venus was perfect. Beautiful. Tough. She'd be wild in bed, too. J.C. could sense it.

You're going to lose your job over this.

Maybe he could get to know her. Accidentally ran into her when she went for lunch or grocery shopping. Maybe she jogged in the afternoon to keep up such a tight body.

Tyler is going to be furious you're here. Instead of doing your damn job.

J.C. scrunched down as far as he could in his seat when she came out, a pet carrier in one hand and a duffle bag in the other. She was going somewhere.

Oh, no. With the death of strippers, maybe her friends, she's getting out. She's going to run. Start somewhere else. I'll never see her again, he thought.

He watched her put the duffle bag and her cat into her vehicle, admiring the shape of her ass. Panicking she was going to drive out of his life.

If he'd been smarter, he would've figured out a way to track her movements. This was all so new to him. The way he felt about her. The rush of thinking about them being together.

If she drives away I can get into her apartment and snoop around. Figure out where she's headed, J.C. thought. *Maybe she left her computer open or something. She only had a bag and her cat. She isn't moving out. She's getting away for a night. Maybe a week. She'll be back.*

Except he didn't want to wait a week to see her again.

Did she have a boyfriend? A woman that hot had a man in her life. Probably some asshole who had three percent body fat. A dumb bodybuilder with zero charisma. Or some older rich guy. Maybe she had daddy issues and only dated men who could wine and dine her. The finer things in life.

When she pulled out of her parking spot and started driving out of the lot, he felt he had no choice but to follow. If she was going across town he could always double back and go through her apartment. The thought of being in her private space got him hard. He could go through her underwear drawer. Maybe take something home. Maybe go through her dirty laundry and find a thong she'd worn all night.

J.C. kept far back, her car in sight at all times.

His phone rang again and he reluctantly answered.

"Where are you? I've been sweating my ass off working," Tyler said. "Are you sleeping?"

J.C. laughed, trying to act casual. "No. I had some personal stuff to attend to this morning. I thought I told you. Dentist appointment. Leaving there now, but then I have to go to the DMV. Last day to do this."

There was a pause on the line. Tyler wasn't stupid. He'd know something wasn't right. He was too good a cop to not see the lies.

J.C. groaned. "Uh, also… I met a woman last night. We didn't sleep much, if you know what I mean. I had to drop her off at her car. Time flies when you're having fun."

Tyler laughed. "Please tell me it wasn't a stripper from the club."

I wish. "No. Woman I met in a bar. Might be more than a one-night stand. Supposed to have dinner with her tonight, too."

"Fine. Go have your fun. Don't worry about me sweating my ass off. I'll call you if anything important comes up. Answer your damn phone," Tyler said.

J.C. hung up and exhaled. That was close. Too close.

He was following her out of Las Vegas and beginning to worry. What if her bag was packed with outfits because she was heading to Reno or Los Angeles to work for a few nights?

All he could do is keep following the woman of his dreams and hope he came up with a game plan to become her man.

Chapter Fourteen

Minnie decided to spend the rest of her little vacation in her room. She had searched her room and was finally convinced she was alone, except for the hateful little fur demon she loved with every fiber of her being. The masseuse would come to her room, as would the other spa technicians, but she resented the fact that she wasn't comfortable leaving her room. Fear made her angry, and she had a hard time controlling her impulses when she was angry. A weakness she didn't like to admit, she needed to feel in control at all times. Fear had the potential to make her feel out of control and helpless. She was neither of those things.

After the car she had seen outside Unique's apartment, Minnie had been fighting a nagging paranoia. She had thought that it may have been cops poking around, but she couldn't help but wonder now if it had been someone else. She kept such a low profile, and had no interest in dating. When she needed the occasional dick, she fucked a random guy in a hotel room and promptly blocked his number. Minnie had no desire for any relationship what-so-ever. Jeff was all the man she needed in her life.

A few years ago, she had a customer that became persistent in pursuing her, it didn't seem like much of a big deal at first. He started coming into the club almost every night she worked, then every night she worked. Soon, he was so demanding of her time that she had to refuse to dance for him anymore. Of course that only made things worse, eventually the management had to 86 him altogether. It should have ended there, but it didn't.

Minnie was forced to turn the tables on the poor lovesick guy. She started to follow him, and soon discovered he was no innocent strip club customer. She was able to, at least loosely, connect him to several stalking and sexual assault victims. Not enough evidence to stand up in a court of law of course, but that's why she did what she did. Where cops and strip club management failed, she succeeded. Her former customer was found with a single gunshot wound to the head in his own garage. He was even considerate enough to have laid out a tarp. An open and shut case, the guy kept his gun in a locked cabinet, and was known to have had a fixation on several ladies who didn't return his affections. The world was a better place without him.

Minnie's masseuse was unable to soften her tensions, and the harder she tried to shake off the thought that someone had come into her room, the thoughts persisted. *He must have come in right after I left for the pool.* A thought suddenly pierced her mind, *the guy at the pool.* She closed her eyes and tried to picture his face, but it wouldn't come. Ever since she was little she had trouble with faces. She seemed to forget them as soon as she saw them. It took at least 3 or 4 visits with a repeat customer before she remembered them. She had to act like she knew everyone she talked to in the club because she had re-introduced herself to several regulars. Nothing ruins a guy's fantasy like the girl he is so taken with can't remember his face or name.

She concentrated all her focus on the man at the pool, young, kinda dorky. *Dorky.* Holy fuckballs! Could it be the same dorky cop she saw at the club? The one eye fucking her from across the room? Had that fucker followed her here? It started to make sense. His behavior when she refused to entertain his small talk was typical of a man who thinks he's in charge, and then discovers he isn't. She was now furious with herself for not bringing her computer.

The burning question in her mind now were his intentions. She expected some cops to be sniffing around the club. They'd be negligent if they weren't. Frank didn't really count of course, he may have been a cop at one point, but now the only thing he seemed to be investigating with any gusto was the bottom of a bottle and the local greasy spoon. Minnie now wondered if the dorky cop she thought was trying to scope out the club because of the murders may have become enamored with her instead. If that turned out to be the case, things would not end well for him.

A seething rage boiled up in her, but she insisted on driving it down. She had never taken out a cop. The fact that he was involved in the investigation of the murders at the club made things especially tricky. Although, she was only responsible for one of them. *Right? Just one of them.* She refused to entertain that invasive thought and stuffed it back into the dark depths of her mind from where it came from.

She had a particularly troubling dilemma here. She knew through her sources that this guy was new and working with Frank's old partner. *Frank.* That guy just kept popping up, didn't he? Despite the fact that he seemed like a decent guy, she knew he had been forcibly retired for doing some shady shit. Almost all cops were into something sketchy at some point in their careers. The job paid like shit, she knew, they were always shitty tippers. She believed most may have started out well intended, but the incentive to exploit their positions got the better of most of them. Of course, some were just shitty to begin with. Rare was the cop who remained pure throughout their tenure. Frank was far from pure, but she didn't think he was an asshole. This other cop however, she now thought definitely was an asshole, a dorky stalker asshole.

Now that she felt like she had a grasp on who and what she was dealing with, her mind eased a little. He wouldn't dare try to confront her again here, but she still felt like it was still a good idea to hang out in her room, she had a pedicure scheduled in an hour anyway. She would resist the urge to run back to her apartment and try to enjoy the rest of her time here. It really was a beautiful place, although she suspected Jeff would beg to differ.

When she returned home she would start to look for the dirty shit the dorky cop was involved with, what was his name? She knew she had run across it at some point, but it escaped her at the moment. She remembered him tipping her on stage and had quite the wad in his hand. She would be willing to bet that it didn't come from his meager salary. He had quite the bulge in his pants as well. While awkward boners were her specialty, they usually held out until the VIP room. She hadn't lap danced for this guy that she could remember. She'd be surprised if he came in for a dance now, but maybe he would think she wouldn't remember him from their brief encounter at the pool. She'd remember him now. Poor guy.

She started to drift off as she lay on the bed in her room. She was dreaming of being covered in a luxurious but weighty mink stole that smells vaguely of, oh what is that? Tuna? The soft knock on the door brought her back to the reality of Jeff crouching between her boobs staring into her face with a look of malice that only a cat owner could love.

Chapter Fifteen

Frank had friends in low places, and it didn't get any lower than the basement of the Las Vegas Police Department.

"Harry McKinley, you old bastard. I figured you'd died years ago and they stuffed your sorry ass and stood you in the corner," Frank said with a smile.

Harry frowned. "How'd you get down here?"

"I still have some connections. Why are you still down here?"

Harry shrugged his shoulders and sat down behind his desk, overloaded with envelopes. "Thanks to you, this is my life. My retirement years. Spent logging packages of evidence no one upstairs is smart enough to use to convict a criminal. I heard they forced you out finally."

"I went kicking and screaming, though." Frank sighed. "I've apologized a hundred times, Harry. I really am sorry you got involved in that mess back then. I told you to stay out of it."

"Water under the bridge." Harry ran his fingers through what was left of his hair. "This isn't a social call. What do you need me to do?"

"The stripper murders. I need to see the evidence."

Harry shook his head. "No can do, buddy. Even if I wanted to, and I don't want to. Officer Fitt, who replaced me nicely once you ruined my career, has it all upstairs."

Frank frowned. "He can't do that."

"Ongoing investigation. Of course he can."

Frank didn't want to involve Tyler in this. He wanted to look at the evidence himself without Tyler looking over his shoulder and see what he could find. Gus Santonelli and his boys were going to need some information sooner than later. They didn't seem like the kind of men who had patience.

Dead strippers are bad for business. Frank knew it was also bad for his own health.

"I appreciate the information," Frank said and took out his wallet. He dropped a twenty on the counter and turned to leave.

Harry laughed. "Once again, the great Frank Michi thinks money can buy everything. You think a twenty is going to make us even? I was bumped down to nothing. I'll die in this dark, filthy box before I can retire. My wife left me. My kids don't even speak to me anymore. I guess I should thank you for taking the blame, but upstairs knew I was involved in some way."

Frank didn't say a word, there was nothing to say to Harry to make him happy. Frank had royally screwed the man, and he did feel sorry about it. It wasn't ever going to be water under the bridge. Harry was pissed and for good reason.

"You want me to take it then? Would that make you feel better?" Frank asked.

Harry crossed his arms and looked away.

Frank left the twenty and snuck out, going in through the front door of the police station.

The officer at the desk obviously knew who he was, because he frowned as soon as Frank opened his mouth and asked if Tyler Fitt was in.

A few minutes later Tyler came out, took Frank by the arm, and led him into the parking lot. "What's up?"

Frank smiled. "You couldn't be seen with me inside. Right?"

"Very much so. I'm knee deep in cases and my partner has decided to disappear on me. If you're asking to buy me lunch, I'm busy."

"I'd usually ask you to take me to lunch," Frank said. "I was trying to find a way to beat around the bush on this, but that's not my style."

"Your style is bulldozing through everything." Tyler grinned. "How's that working out for you, old partner?"

"I just saw Harry. He's still mad."

"I'm surprised he didn't use an evidence weapon to shoot you in the head and then bury you in a manila envelope down there. No one would ever find your body."

Frank waved a hand. "I need to look at the files for the dead strippers."

"Why?"

"I can't say."

Tyler shrugged. "You know I can't help you. No matter what I wouldn't. Any screw-up in these cases and my badge and gun are taken away. You are definitely not worth sinking to your level."

"I guess I deserved that." Frank shrugged. "Buy me dinner tonight?"

"Not a chance. Who are you working for now? Obviously, you poking your nose in this isn't because you care about a couple of strippers." Tyler let out a big breath. "Please tell me you're not involved with Santonelli and his crew."

"Who?"

"Liar. Frank… they'll kill you if you don't find out what they want to know. Hell, they'll kill you if you give them everything they want. Has it even occurred to you they're setting you up? They're just as likely to be the murderers."

"I don't think so. My gut tells me they need smiling and breathing strippers to make money," Frank said. "This is also bad for business. Another dead stripper so close to the other two and we got us a serial killer who hates hot chicks."

"The two cases are unrelated."

Frank laughed again. "I know you don't really believe that. They are definitely connected. And there will be more of them."

Tyler took a step toward Frank. "How do you know? You got a confession you need to give me?"

"I'm too lazy to kill anyone and too fat and old to try to attack a stripper," Frank said. "They'd all kick my ass. I have no delusion I could go more than a minute with one of them, either. I'm on your side. Trying to figure this out, too. Make me a paid informant. I'll hit the streets and see what I can shake out."

Tyler shook his head. "You a C.I. in this town? Not gonna happen. Everyone knows you, knows you used to be a crooked cop, and knows not to talk to you."

"You just called me a crooked ex-cop."

"Because you are," Tyler said.

"Exactly. Who better to get information than someone like me? It's perfect. I can do the things you can't legally do." Frank smiled. "The things I used to do to get everyone in trouble. Now I'm on my own."

"You are your worst enemy. What do you want for this help?"

"A typical fee you'd pay any C.I. these days. I know the going rates. I'll need some walking around money, of course." Frank put his hand out.

"Nope. I do things by the book now. I'll put in a ticket for a payment… when you bring me something I can use. Anything about the two murders, and if you get wind of a third. And we both know there will be a third death related to this."

"Sounds like a plan. Now… are you going to buy me dinner?"

Tyler turned and walked away, shaking his head.

Chapter Sixteen

Minnie's pedicure was as expected, fabulous. She didn't enjoy it like she should have, however. Her mind wouldn't let go of the man she now suspected of following her, the dorky young cop. She remembered seeing him at the club several times now, and she had finally remembered his name, J.C. He was ass-deep into the murders at the club and apparently now smitten with her. A part of her pitied the poor rookie cop turned stalker, as she now understood she would have to deal with him.

They hadn't connected the two murders at the club as of yet, but she suspected that the big boss' from back east would soon change that. Those guys had a vested interest in solving or at least stopping any more killing of their livestock. While losing a little competition might have been advantageous for Minnie, the murders were certainly bad for the mob cash cow and the obvious but overlooked laundering operation. They would be pushing for a quick end to this investigation and the easiest way to do that would be to connect the two dead strippers and tie the whole thing up neat and quick. Catching the actual killer of the women didn't matter much, as long as there weren't any more. The cops sniffing around were much more of an issue than a dead stripper or two.

Minnie was anxious to get back home and to her laptop where she could find out more information on this J.C. guy. The anxiety only served to fuel her anger toward her new admirer; she was going to like taking him out. She still had one more night booked here and forced herself to stay, if only to prove that she had the willpower to overcome her emotional response. She ordered a rich cream sauced pasta from room service which was bad for her ass but great for her nerves and tried to focus on the book she brought.

Although it was a mental feast of the walking dead with plenty of blood and gore, she just couldn't quite get into it. Eventually she gave up and lay down on the bed. Jeff, having been satiated, lay at her feet. No point in cuddling when he didn't need anything from her. He was such a dick, and she loved him so.

She didn't quite sleep, but found herself instead in that strange state between awareness and slumber. Her thoughts were a mixture of dreams and memories, where the line between reality and fantasy was as clear as a stage full of fake smoke. Her fist was striking something not quite hard but not quite soft either. Over and over she rained furious blows on this unknown object and when it stopped making noise and stopped moving she continued to hit it again and again. After becoming aware of the warm splatter that had landed on her face, she finally stopped. She looked down at the object of her fury and had an odd sense of recognition. She noticed this object had hair that just happened to be the same color as Sass'. Minnie snapped back into the room, she ran to the suite's bathroom and vomited. *Well at least it won't stick to my ass,* she thought sickly. Jeff lifted his head in annoyance at the sound, but stayed where he was.

Still reeling from this revelation she limped back to the bed and sat on the edge. Jeff gave her a look of death. He got up to rub his head against her, but only briefly. He wouldn't want to give her the impression that he cared more than just a little. She was trying to remember the night that Sass was killed. Most of it was a bit of a blank, just an ordinary night she had thought. One of many, nothing special about it at all, and yet she was now sure that she had killed the young stripper. Had she been angry with her about something? Sass could be a bit of a pill sometimes, but she couldn't think of a reason for wanting her dead. Minnie had always taken pride in ridding the world of vermin that either had already hurt people or had the potential to. She exclusively killed bad people therefore Sass must have been bad.

She wouldn't describe them as black outs, but this wasn't the only time where a chunk of time had gone missing. Sometimes she would realize that she couldn't remember bits and pieces of certain events. It had never really concerned her however. Who remembers everything, what was she, an elephant? The one time she found herself alarmed, was when she woke up to discover the neighbor's small dog under her bed. It was dead and appeared to have been strangled. The yappy little thing had been a point of contention between her parents and the neighbors next door because the damn thing would never shut up. Minnie remembered being irritated by the thing, but had wished it no ill will. Her concern over the incident had not been that she had killed it, but that someone had planted it there in order to incriminate her. These neighbors had once suggested to her parents that it might be a good idea for her to *talk to someone.* As if. She may have been a little introverted, but she was far from crazy. She simply put the damned thing out in the can with the rest of the garbage and moved on. The world was a little less noisy now.

Sass must have done something or been preparing to do something evil. There was no other logical explanation. Maybe she blocked it out because she had a bit of a soft spot for the girl? Of course, that made the most sense. Anyway she was dead now, and Minnie understood that she deserved it. Now the issue was how to deal with it. She couldn't now rule out the possibility that the cops might put the two killings together, and that presented a problem for her and the cops.

It was still a few hours until her designated check out time, but the sun was up. Minnie gathered her things and used the lint roller to pick up any cat hairs that Jeff may have left behind. She didn't want to leave a trace of her hairy minion. Or, was she his? She liked to leave a clean room for the maids as well. It seemed like a shitty job that didn't need to be made any shittier. She gathered her things, including Jeff, and deposited them in her car before proceeding to the front desk to return her key. She moved quickly and didn't say anything as she did, aware that J.C. the dork may be watching. She thought she would be able to tell if he was, but he was almost certainly trained in surveillance. That fact made her doubt her own abilities to detect if someone were watching her, which made her want to kill him even more. It scared her, and she wanted him to hurt for it.

She drove too fast on the way home. Every time she told herself to slow down, she only did for a moment or two before she noticed herself speeding again. Getting pulled over right now would be a very bad thing. She took a moment to ponder if J.C. could pull her over, but let it go immediately. He wasn't that kind of cop. She fantasized about how she would like to take him out. Maybe he could eat a bullet like her other stalker? He could hang himself? Even better, he could *accidentally* die while choking himself as he jerked off. *Erotic asphyxiation*, she thought as a smile crossed her face. The smile retreated as she thought about the implications of the death of a cop who was in the middle of a seedy murder investigation. If anyone had even the slightest whiff of foul play instead of a masturbation mishap that would only make things worse. *Fuck.* She might not get to kill this guy after all. She had really started to have her heart set on him getting found with a belt around his neck and his dick in his hand. She reminded herself to tuck that little gem of a method away for another deserving victim.

No, the best thing might be to pin the damn murders on the dork himself. She had never framed anyone before, but she had little doubt about her ability to do so. She would need to find a motive for him to do it and evidence to point in his direction. Maybe his mommy was a whore and he had issues with it? Or a girl once laughed at his pecker? This was new territory and she wasn't quite sure how to proceed despite her confidence. She would need to be careful, and she would need to get as much information on the rookie cop as possible. She needed to get to her computer. Minnie began to speed again.

Chapter Seventeen

Steve was getting his knob polished by one of the new girls from Reno he'd had to fly in. She might not be a great dancer but she could suck the chrome off of a trailer hitch. He made a mental note to keep her around as long as possible, not an easy feat when the bitches in the dressing room told the new girls about a serial killer taking out strippers.

The cost of shipping new asses in was going to get him in trouble, too. While Mister Santonelli understood running a strip club meant actually having strippers on the stage and in the VIP room, the added costs were not good.

As if on cue, and while Steve was so distracted thinking about Santonelli and money he wasn't paying attention to the new girl, the double knock on the door made him frown.

It could only mean one thing: Gus Santonelli and his thugs were in the building.

"Stop. Get up," Steve said, pushing her away. She fell to the floor and looked pissed. "Get back to work. I'll make sure you get an extra tip, honey."

"My name isn't Honey, it's Sapphire." She got up and put a hand out. "I want to get paid now."

Steve shook his head and stood, zipping up. "My boss is about to enter through that door. He's not a good person. Nor does he care if you blew me and I told you I'd pay you later."

"What? I ain't a hooker, you small dick jerkoff." Sapphire put her hands on her hips. "You pay me or I tell him you stiffed me. Then we'll see how good he is."

The door opened and Gus Santonelli walked in, looking amused.

"Sorry. Am I interrupting?" Gus asked.

Steve shook his head and stared at Sapphire. "No, boss. She was just leaving. She has customers to see to."

"I see." Gus smiled at Sapphire. "Well, ma'am, I'll get out of your way. Good luck out there. Looks like a lot of tourists with bulging wallets."

Sapphire was staring at Steve.

Please, bitch, leave, Steve thought. *Walk out and don't make a scene.*

"Sorry to bother you, Steve's boss, but he owes me some money," Sapphire said.

Steve closed his eyes.

"Is this true, Steve?" Gus asked.

Steve opened his eyes and saw the amusement on Santonelli's face and the two goons standing on either side of the doorway.

"Yes, but I can explain," Steve said.

Santonelli put up his hand and turned toward the stripper. "I'm sorry… how rude of me. I'm Mister Santonelli but friends call me Gus. What's your name, honey?"

"Sapphire, not Honey."

Gus shook his head. "Not your stage name, dear. I mean your actual name."

The girl hesitated. She looked at Steve, who looked away. He wasn't going to help this bitch now.

"Your name," Gus said, an edge to his voice. "Surely you filled out some official forms when you showed up today. You do have a driver's license. No?" Gus stepped back and looked her up and down. "I mean, no ID on you unless it's stuck between your drooping fake tits or your fat bubble butt."

"Fuck you," Sapphire said. She looked at Steve for support, as if it was going to happen.

Gus Santonelli laughed. "You must be new. I like your spunk, Sapphire. How much does he owe you for your services?"

"Uh, I mean… I'm not a pro or anything. I was just, uh, helping him out. He hinted at an extra tip and all."

Gus snapped his fingers and one of his men stepped forward, took out a wad of cash, and peeled off a few twenties. He handed them to Gus, who reached out with them to the stripper.

When Sapphire went to take the money, Gus pulled it back. "Not so fast. This is a hundred dollars. Surely, Steve here doesn't have a dick worth that much." He glanced back over his shoulder. "But my two men are definitely worth it. Follow them to the limo but hurry up. I want that ass up on the stage in fifteen minutes or I drag you out in front of everyone. Got it?"

Before she could react, Steve grabbed her arm and handed her off to the two smiling goons, who led her away.

"Sorry, boss," Steve said, looking at the floor.

"You owe me the hundred and interest."

"Of course," Steve said. "What can I help you with, boss? This is a pleasant surprise having you back so soon."

"Get used to it. I'm sticking around town until they find this killer. Some of the other managers are getting nervous. Losing business is always hard." Santonelli moved past Steve and sat down at his desk. "I'm wondering why you're not more worried."

"I am. I definitely am," Steve said. He felt the sweat running down the side of his face. "I made a mistake, boss. Blowing off a little steam was all."

"You know what your problem has always been? Your lack of focus. You never see the big picture, Steve. You're too busy taking advantage of what I've worked so hard for." Santonelli put his feet up on the desk and put his hands behind his neck. "Forcing desperate strippers to blow you, skimming cash off the top each night and creating problems for me."

Steve shook his head. "No. Not at all, boss. You got that all wrong. I'm not doing any of those things. I mean, yeah, an occasional blowjob never hurt anybody."

"I beg to differ. Do you realize what I should do right now? Any clue?"

Steve thought about it, but everything he stopped on was a dark and negative thing, so he finally shook his head.

"If it wasn't for a killer on the loose, I'd already have dragged you out back and shot you twice in the head. Personally done it, too. You know why?"

When it was obvious to Steve his boss was waiting for an answer, he cleared his throat. "I don't."

"Sure you do, Steve. I just told you the three things you're doing wrong. Aren't you listening to me? Should I add your lack of understanding to the list, too?" Santonelli shook his head. "You have two choices. You can either do your fucking job and leave me to work on the big picture problems, or I take you out to the desert and dump you in one of the many pre-dug holes. Which do you prefer?"

"I'm sorry, boss. I'll do better. I promise."

Santonelli smiled. "Perfect. Do me a favor. Go get me a shot and a beer. Be quick about it, too."

Steve did as he was told, wiping his face on a bar rag as he snapped at the bartender, Cinnamon, to hurry it up.

The two thugs came back into the club and followed Steve into the office. Steve noticed Sapphire, looking dejected, was heading to the stage.

"Thanks, Steve," Santonelli said, but didn't touch the drinks. "Those are for you."

"I don't understand."

Santonelli nodded at the two thugs, who grabbed Steve and slammed him against the desk. His desk. They yanked his left hand onto the desk and held it in place.

"No, no, boss, don't do this. I'm sorry I said I was sorry I said I wasn't going to do it anymore it was a few girls a few dollars I'll pay it all back I'm not going to screw up anymore..."

Santonelli had a knife in his hand and was smiling. "Like I said, you screwed up with three things. Forcing strippers to have sex with you. Stealing my cash. Creating problems. You know what that means? Anyone can answer."

The thug holding Steve's quivering hand spoke up. "It means three digits."

"Exactly. Vinnie knows the rules. Notice he has all of his digits, Steve? Now... and listen carefully to the question... Do you want three different fingers cut, or a finger and a half? Really up to you. Since I can't kill you and dump you out back with the cops constantly lurking about, this is the next best thing. Of course, if you cross me again, I'll have no choice. I need a manager right now, even if it's for the police. No time to train a new guy, and raise suspicions."

Steve started to scream but the other thug put a meaty hand on his mouth.

"I'll ask again... one and a half fingers or three different ones?"

Steve wanted to pass out as Gus Santonelli decided one and a half fingers made more sense.

Chapter Eighteen

Minnie got back to her apartment in the early afternoon, and after freeing Jeff from the confines of his carrier she booted up her computer. She began looking for as much information on J.C. as she could find. Not much, as it so happened. She found his address and a few other things, but nothing that really stood out. Typical stuff for a rookie cop. His partner who happened to be Frank's ex-partner didn't have too much going on either. Although she knew he was probably involved in the same stuff that took Frank out, which meant that J.C. was probably on the take as well. All of this was really just supposition on her part though, didn't help her much in this case.

Her main objective was to get this dorky stalker rookie cop off her tail. She needed to put this goofy Romeo out of commission both as her stalker and off the dead stripper case. She found nothing in his background or online footprint that would help her. Next she thought she would see where they were in the investigations. The only thing connecting the two murders was that the women both worked at the same club. That was it. Both method and motivation seemed unrelated. She wasn't on any of the cop's radar. She congratulated herself on that point, but at the same time was disappointed at the lack of evidence in both cases. She had nothing to plant on J.C., no way to connect him to either murder. Killing him as appealing as it was, she pictured his swollen self strangled face, was not an option. She once again had to temper her disappointment. Minnie decided she would need to kill another stripper from the club, but this time she would make sure she left a trail that would lead back to J.C.. She would need to do it soon though, the quicker this was over, the better.

But who deserved to die? It appeared she wasn't as discerning as she once thought she was when it came to her victims. She was convinced that Cass had needed to go, but the fact that she had blocked it out tugged at the back of her mind. She had done something that appeared to be outside of her conscious thought, and that unnerved her. It made her feel that she only had the illusion of control over her emotions and actions. Up until the realization at the retreat, Minnie had never doubted her motivations or noble intentions for killing. These thoughts made her uncomfortable, and she decided to put them away. She was the fucking hero. The badass who took out the bad people, she would never believe otherwise.

When Minnie finally looked up from her laptop, she noticed two things. First she was starving, second it was getting late and she was on the schedule tonight. It was Friday and bound to be busy and lucrative. She noticed one more thing. Jeff was staring at her with his signature *feed me or die* look. She got up to handle him first. She would be rendered useless if her cat decided to actually murder her. She opened him a can of his favorite disgusting wet mess and filled his kibble bowl. His water dish was an expensive fountain that featured constantly running filtered water. He only drank out of the toilet.

Her kitchen was a little low on human food. Her cat food stockpile was always well stocked due to the constant fear of death by an ornery furball, so she ordered from her favorite Thai place. Tom Ka soup and Pad Ginger with shrimp. When it arrived she ate with gusto but slowly. If she ate too fast she would end up with an upset tummy at work. She was quite adept at framing her bouncers for the unladylike consequences of eating too quickly, but avoiding it all together was always a better way to go. Although one time she was able to place the blame on poor pathetic Steve, no one would expect a foul cloud to come out of a hot ass like hers with that greasy piece of shit around. It made her smile to think of it, but alas she needed to get ready for work. She had masturbation to inspire, a dirty stripper to kill, and a cop to frame. It was going to be a fun night.

She took a shower, and then blow dried her hair but left it unstyled. She had just enough time to close her eyes for a short but desperately needed nap. Night shifts in Vegas rarely ended before the sun came up, and she didn't want to rely solely on energy drinks or blow as many of the other girls did. She needed actual rest which came a little easier than expected. She usually slept poorly when she was unsure of her next move, but she had a good idea of how she was going to proceed. She woke feeling refreshed and ready for the night and the horny men drunk on Vegas and alcohol that were probably already waiting for her. She put on her makeup, finished her hair, and headed out into the neon lit night.

When she got to the club, it was already buzzing, as were all of the patrons. *Perfect,* she thought. Minnie liked them drunk, but not too drunk. They needed to be able to remember using their credit cards, just lucid enough to be unable to dispute the charges. On her way to the dressing room, Steve looked somehow worse than usual with a large bandage on one hand. Minnie briefly considered asking him what happened, but then she remembered she didn't care. Although she made a mental note of it, it was a little odd.

She opened the dressing room door to the usual mind numbingly stupid banter about nothing important at all. She went to open her locker, which wasn't technically hers, but everyone knew she used it. When she opened the door, a large pink duffle bag fell forward and bonked her on the head. Almost immediately a stripper she hadn't seen before said "Oh my God! I'm so sorry! I haven't got a lock yet. I'm Sapphire by the way." The newbie held out her hand with acrylic claws painted the same stupid shade of pink as the duffle bag.

"Ha ha! I'm Venus, nice to meet you! No worries, but it's a good idea to get a lock soon so no one steals your stuff, and knows that the locker is in use. This is the locker that I usually use," Minnie said, and was pleased at how well she had hidden her fury and utter contempt for this person. With her bad boob job and floppy ass, this chick was probably giving $20 blow jobs to every Tom, Dick, and hairier Dick. Man, they were getting desperate. She knew that the rumors of the murders were flying around scaring off the new hires.

"Wow, you're so pretty. Here let me move my bag. I'll find another locker," Sapphire sang in a sugary sweet tone. Minnie despised her with every fiber of her being. She knew almost instantly, that not only was this girl bad for business, she would be bad for the other girls as well. Anyone who spoke in that disingenuous tone was obviously up to no good, probably a thief in addition to a cheap hooker. She was pleased at not only her ability to pick out bad people, but that she now knew who to get rid of. She had her mark.

Venus took to the stage raking it in to one of her favorite songs *I want to fuck you to death* by Huntress. An obscure song, but a crowd pleaser just the same. She didn't have time to gather her tips from the basket the bouncer had put them in because she had customers lined up already for the VIP room. She asked the meathead to hold on to them for her. She was known for tipping her staff generously and that bought her respect, trust, and loyalty. She had no doubt that every single dollar (a few twenties too) would be there when she got back. He knew he would be rewarded handsomely and would likely even return them to her stacked and faced like a good boy.

She returned from the VIP room sweaty and in dire need of a drink of water and a fresh piece of gum. The last guy insisted on having the well chewed piece of big red in her mouth, for a nice tip of course. After a quick trip to her newly reclaimed locker, she went back out to the floor. Standing in a dark corner she noticed the dorky cop. He wasn't in a silly pink shirt like last time, but she could tell he was trying to blend in. He wasn't succeeding, but still managed to look like a dork. She wasn't sure if he had seen her or not, but he probably knew she was there. Her name was on the white board at the front which displayed all the dancers currently working each shift. Venus quickly moved out of his view. She spotted Sapphire standing by the bar looking perplexed and lost. *Fuck, this is too perfect,* she thought. She walked up to the new girl and asked, "How is your night going?"

"Not that great," Sapphire whined. "This isn't at all like Reno."

"Vegas is a tough beast, but you'll get used to it. I promise," Venus said.

"Yeah, I guess," Sapphire said. "But I think I'm almost ready to go home."

Venus noticed that the young girl with the botched boobs was wearing a ridiculous amount of glitter. *Sweet baby Jesus, this just keeps getting better.* "I tell you what: see that guy over there in the corner?" Venus gave a slight nod in J.C.'s direction. "How about I give you a hundred dollars to go dance for him? Tell him it's from a secret admirer. If he really likes you, he'll get more dances. If not, you'll get a little more experience under your belt."

"Wow, really? Why would you do that?" Sapphire looked at the hundred dollar bill Venus was holding out like it was the first one she'd ever seen. This girl was an idiot, an evil one no doubt.

"We really need girls with all the rumors going around, and some doofus just gave me that bill for the wad of gum in my mouth," Venus said, trying to mimic Sapphire's sweet tone. She wasn't sure she nailed it, but it was close enough.

The evil idiot took the bill and tucked it into her little stripper purse and tottered over to the dorky cop. He looked a little puzzled, but followed her to the VIP, where he would surely end up with a whole lot of soon to be dead stripper glitter on his person. If she was lucky, probably a strand or two of her hair as well. If somehow that failed, the two would be on at least two or three of the cameras in the club. That may have been the best hundred she had ever spent, a much better value than the cat water fountain.

Venus was so busy for the rest of her shift that she managed to avoid both J.C. and Sapphire for the rest of the night. Too bad Sapphire couldn't say the same. The club closed shortly before sunrise and Minnie watched Sapphire (who she now only thought of as the *Evil Idiot*) get into an Uber and head to her shitty first floor apartment.

She parked a block away, and padded quietly up to the sliding glass door on the back patio. It was locked, but not secured with any other device. Minnie used a small screwdriver she kept in her car (because you never know), to pry the door upward from the bottom. She tilted the door just a touch which released the latch, and slid easily inside. The Evil Idiot was already snoring slightly, clothed only in the glitter she had on at work. She opened her eyes only when Minnie drew the knife across her throat. She made no sound, and Minnie left the way she came.

Minnie made a small detour on her way home to J.C.'s home, located his car, and smeared the tiniest amount of the Evil Idiot's blood under the handle of the driver's side door. As the sun began to rise, she deposited the knife she had used in a nearby dumpster. When she got back to her own home, she burned the gloves she had been wearing in her sink while Jeff eyed her from the kitchen floor, half starved to death. She fed the damned thing and slunk into her own bed to sleep the sleep of heroes.

Chapter Nineteen

Tyler thought of himself as a good cop. Not a great one. Not a hero. Just a good cop. He didn't really care what his title was, either. It was all the same. Wearing the uniform as a beat cop or a suit as a detective still meant doing the best job he could do.

Sure, he'd skimmed here and there. He'd looked the other way a couple of times. He'd kept his mouth shut when Frank had gone down. It was all part of the job.

All in all, Tyler Fitt was a good cop who knew his shit.

He knew something was off with his partner, J.C., right now, too.

They'd gotten the call to Bette Chamblin's apartment as the sun was going down. A neighbor had complained about a weird smell.

"Bette? She doesn't look like a Betty," Tyler had remarked, staring at the dead, naked stripper on the bed in a pool of her blood. "Must be a family name."

J.C. didn't comment, too busy staring at the dead woman.

Tyler punched his partner's shoulder. "What's the matter? You never seen big, fake tits before?"

"Uh, yeah, I have." J.C. looked like he was going to be sick.

"What's gotten into you today?" Tyler had noticed J.C. had been off since they'd gotten the call and walked into the crime scene. Thanks to the nosy neighbor across the hall, an old man who was obviously keeping tabs on the stripper, who went by the name Sapphire, she'd been found before she really began to stink.

Tyler left J.C. staring and went across the hall to Mister Winters, who might be fifty but looked ten years older. Drinking and drugs hadn't been kind to the man.

"What did you see?" Tyler asked.

"See? Nothin'." Winters looked down at his feet. His apartment was a mess. The guy might even be a hoarder, although the junk was mostly old VHS tapes, stacked in piles around the sixty-inch television. The only real thing of value in the place.

Tyler picked up a box and shook his head. Swedish Erotica. It looked like the entire series, which might be hundreds of tapes. The guy was into porn. Like all guys. Except this guy was a collector of the vintage stuff.

"How long have you been watching her, Mister Winters?" Tyler asked. He walked to the front door, closed it and stared out through the peephole. "You get a clear view of her stripper ass when she gets home from work every morning. That must get you off."

"No, it ain't like that," Winters said. "She's only been here a couple of days. I helped her move in, like a good neighbor does."

Tyler smiled. "If I go through your shit, what's the chance I'll find a pair of her sparkly thongs hidden away, covered in your DNA?"

Winters was staring at his feet again. "It ain't like that. She gave me a pair for helpin' her. I swear."

"Easy enough to ask her," Tyler said and then frowned and snapped his fingers. "Oh, no, wait… she's dead. That's inconvenient."

Tyler was a good cop. He knew this idiot hadn't killed her. He'd jerked off looking at her, though. He'd definitely stolen a couple of pairs of her dirty undies and wrapped them around his small pecker each night.

But my gut says he didn't kill her, Tyler thought. "Get dressed, Mister Winters. We'll need to take you downtown for a proper interview. Make sure we don't miss anything, like if she had a boyfriend. Maybe a girlfriend."

Mister Winters grins at Tyler but then realizes he's not making a joke. He stands and heads for the bedroom.

Tyler points at a cop he doesn't know. "Follow him. Make sure he doesn't pull a weapon or tries to escape."

The cop laughs. "He's not climbing out a window."

"Just the same," Tyler says with a wave. He paces around the room but doesn't see anything obvious except the guy had an unhealthy obsession with porn. There might be thousands of dollars worth of tapes, even though everything is now online and mostly free.

Tyler didn't notice a computer in the apartment. When Mister Winters was led out to a squad car, Tyler did a quick search of the bedroom. No computer but file boxes filled with dirty magazines. Hundreds of them.

J.C. was standing in the parking lot, staring into space.

"What did you do?" Tyler asks, an innocuous question that could also get a rise.

It gets a rise. "I didn't do anything," J.C. mumbles, his face getting red.

"Is there something you want to tell me, kid?" Tyler asks, dropping into cop mode. The Good Cop part of the equation.

J.C. shook his head. "No. I think I saw her dancing the last time we were in the club. That's all. Another dead stripper. What do you think is happening?"

Tyler knew J.C. wasn't telling him everything, but decided to not push it. Not yet. "Isn't it obvious what's going on? Someone hates strippers. I'm sure, in the next year or so, someone will hate prostitutes again. Then the homeless. People can't just be nice to one another. Everyone has an agenda, I guess. We're just here to clean it up, get to the bottom of it." He paused and then grinned. "Figure out the unlikeliest of suspects and toss them in a cell. Throw away the key."

J.C. went white, nodding his head slowly.

"Maybe you should take the rest of the day off," Tyler said, back to Good Cop. "I'll run by the club and find out when she was last working. Sounds like last night."

J.C. walked a few steps and puked on the sidewalk.

A few cops coming and going groaned and stepped around the stinking mess that had been J.C.'s lunch.

"Go home. Get some rest. You don't look so good," Tyler said. "One of the guys will give you a ride back to the station. I have actual police work to do." He didn't wait for an answer, leaving J.C. bent over, hands on knees, waiting for breakfast to exit as well.

Instead of driving straight to the strip club, Tyler went to Frank's apartment.

Frank answered on the third knock, looking like he'd just staggered out of bed despite it being so late. Even after dark, the air was hot, like the streets refused to give the heat back to the sun.

"Another dead stripper," Tyler said and let himself in.

Frank had been drinking, an empty six-pack of cheap beer on the TV tray next to his chair in the living room.

"Please… come in," Frank said.

"Don't mind if I do."

Frank stretched; his eyes bleary. "Are you back to thinking I killed the dancers?"

Tyler shook his head. "When's the last time you ate?"

Frank shrugged.

"Get dressed. We're going to get some dinner. We need to talk."

Frank smiled. "We do?"

"Yeah. I need your help, Frank."

Chapter Twenty

Waking to the sight of a pair of menacing eyes three inches from your face coupled with a heavy sensation on your chest would've scared the holy shit out of most people. But not Minnie. She sighed and pushed Jeff off to the side. She was going to get up anyway, she had to pee. It was already late afternoon and she had slept the better part of twelve hours. Sleeping that long was usually not a good sign for her. She had been putting in some work lately.

Despite the threatening way Jeff was staring at her, even throwing in a low moaning sound to emphasize his displeasure, Minnie started an extra strong pot of coffee before tending to her murderous furball.

"Sorry little fucker, you're going to have to wait," she growled back at him.

She was having a really hard time waking up, and coffee was more important at the moment. She thought about calling off work, but thought it would be a bad idea. She knew that they were starting to get low on dancers with all the murder going around. Because of her reputation of being a no bullshit kind of dancer, it would look weird if she didn't show. She also wanted to know what kind of talk was going around and if anyone was spreading the kind of rumors that might reflect on her. It took her only a brief look at the news to see that Sapphire had been found.

What she hadn't seen was whether any arrests had been made. It seemed unlikely that they had picked up J.C. yet. That would surely make the news. The sooner the better in her opinion. Really she had done the cops, the guys back east, and the club a huge favor as her latest endeavor would tie everything up neatly and end the panic, rumors and suspicion. She had left a clear trail of evidence leading in his direction. It wouldn't be a stretch to wrap him up in all the murders. Even if the cops didn't really think they were all connected, they had plenty of motivation to clear all those murders at the same time.

She had woken so late she didn't have much time to do much but eat, shower and get out the door. It was a weekend night, and the tourists who didn't know or care about the local murders would be ready for a long night of drinking and blue balls. Well, hopefully blue balls, miscalculation would lead to satisfaction, which stops guys from getting more dances. Good thing she took out that hooker masquerading as a stripper before she could really hurt business. Murder might be bad for business, but Minnie took special exception to strippers finishing off customers. You couldn't make money selling blue balls if you had actual hookers in your midst. The briefest flicker of a thought crossed her mind that she hadn't really known if Sapphire had been a customer ruining hooker. She snuffed it out.

She got to work just a tad later than usual, but her usual locker was free. Imagine that. Actually, a lot of lockers were free. This being a weekend night in Vegas, it was a little concerning. Indeed the dressing room was eerily quiet. Minnie heard none of the usual *Where's my bag of drugs* or

I don't really like licking my boyfriend's butthole, but I love him so I do it anyway. The only conversations going on were whispers, almost as if they thought the murderer might be listening. Weird.

When she checked the white board at the front, she saw that the list was down by at least half. She checked herself in with the DJ and he warned her that due to the lack of talent, a lofty word for some, she may get called up on stage more often than usual. Minnie handed him a pre-tip to make sure that didn't happen. Too many stages could impede her lap dance revenue. Next she stopped at the bar, where Cinnamon was running her mouth. At least that was normal.

"I heard the cops think it's a customer," Cinnamon said. Minnie hadn't heard that at all.

"But I think it could be a woman. Think about it. No one would ever suspect a woman, customer or dancer. And women tend to smile in each others' faces while talking shit behind their backs. It makes perfect sense. Maybe some ugly ass stripper is taking out her competition. Or some disgruntled wife or girlfriend pissed that her man is spending too much time and money at the club," Cinnamon blabbered on.

The customer in whose direction she was speaking toward looked unimpressed with her half baked theory. Minnie didn't think he was in fact listening at all. His gaze pointed directly at the stage where a cute but obvious newbie was hanging on to the pole for dear life.

Minnie however was listening. Her gaze was also directed at the stage, but her ears were tuned in to Cinnamon. *Ugh, this bitch.* Killing anyone else connected to the club would be a spectacularly bad idea. Bad idea or not, if they didn't pick up J.C. soon, she may not be left with much of a choice. Although it would be especially treacherous, she thought she could pull it off undetected. She knew that Cinnamon was simply talking out her ass and had no actual knowledge, but she didn't want her to plant that idea in someone's head who might actually decide it was a plausible theory.

It wasn't just the cops that Minnie was concerned about. She knew the real owners of the club had been paying more visits than usual and they were the real danger. Cops could be bought, framed, and killed but those bastards back east didn't fuck around. Nope, they wouldn't just kill you, they'd have fun with you first. Almost like a cat playing with its catch. Now that she thought about it, maybe those guys weren't all bad. Scary as fuck, but she could respect that. She remembered Steve's bandaged hand, and decided there was a likely connection there.

Cinnamon was a popular fixture at the club. People liked her, although Minnie couldn't understand why. Bitch was always talking, and that made her bad for business in her eyes. Not just because of the murders either. Cinnamon had a habit of repeating private conversations and spreading gossip causing drama. Minnie was really regretting not getting rid of her earlier. She wished it had been Cinnamon instead of Cass that she had beaten the literal shit out of. A tactical error on her part. One that should not be repeated.

"Personally, I can think of a lot of girls who might be capable of murder. Women are ruthless and mean."

Now it appeared that Cinnamon was simply talking to the space in front of her. No one was really looking in her direction at all, and yet she persisted.

"What about you Venus? Who would you kill? Not that you would, you're so nice. But I'd bet you've thought about it." Cinnamon was now aiming her blather directly at her. She had to respond. In her head she thought *troublesome blabbermouth bitches,* but aloud she said,

"Well I believe in Karma." She didn't, but she'd known several dancers by that name. "So I think people just get what they have coming. No need to help it along," she said with a warm sticky smile.

Cinnamon seemed satisfied with her answer, but pulled away. Minnie took advantage of the break in the conversation to walk away. The floor was filled with bulging wallets which must be uncomfortable to sit on. Left too long they could even lead to back pain. She needed to do them a favor and relieve them of their burdensome cash. She was after all, a dedicated, if somewhat unconventional, public servant.

Chapter Twenty-One

Frank wasn't here to drink tonight, although it was super tempting. He'd been clean for a few hours and being sober was a nightmare. He nearly did what Tyler had warned him not to do a hundred times last night at the diner and stepped up to Cinnamon with a smile and ordered a drink or four.

Nope. Can't blow this one. Not when Tyler needs my help, Frank thought.

Instead, he kept his distance in the corner, sipping on an overpriced Coke and keeping track of everyone in and out.

Cinnamon and Venus were chatting at the bar for a few before Venus wandered off.

Frank had spent many nights imagining any number of combinations of these girls making out and going down on one another while he got to watch. It was every guy's dream to have a threesome with a couple of hot strippers. As if Frank thought he would last more than a minute. But still…

Steve was wandering around, looking more pissed than normal, his hand bandaged. He looked wired, too. In all the times Frank had seen the club owner, he never looked high.

He always looked annoyed, though. There were never enough customers, never enough booze being sold, never enough strippers to take the money in and keep the customers happy and drinking.

Frank had brought a small pad and pen with him to take notes, but it was too dark in the club. Definitely too dark in his little corner, which was fine with him. He wasn't in the mood to chat with anyone, especially if he were sober.

Cinnamon was watching him and she poured a glass of beer and made a beeline for his table, putting the beer down.

Frank sighed and waved his hand. "I'm not drinking yet. Gotta pace myself, hun."

"This one's on me," Cinnamon said. She glanced back to make sure no one was waiting on a drink before sitting down across from Frank. "Let me know if some drunk needs a refill."

Frank nodded.

Cinnamon seemed to be thinking about something as she stared at Frank.

"What?" He finally asked, uncomfortable. He'd spent many nights making small-talk while staring at her amazing tits and ass, but this seemed different. Like they were about to have a real, adult conversation.

"Is it you, Frank? Please tell me it isn't you."

Frank frowned. "What do you think I did?"

Cinnamon looked over her shoulder again. "Someone connected to the club is killing off the dancers."

"I'm not connected anymore than every other customer in here," Frank said.

She turned back to Frank and smiled faintly. "You're like another piece of furniture. Isn't that what you always say? A night without you at the bar is weird… and tonight it's weird you're hidden in the corner, observing. What are you looking for, Frank? Your next victim?"

Frank scooped up the beer and drank it in one pull, slamming it back down on the table. He licked his lips. Tyler was going to be pissed. "You can't seriously believe I'd kill strippers. I love them. If I killed all of you, what else would I have to do with my life? It doesn't even make sense."

"I'm not a stripper," Cinnamon said defensively.

"You're wasting your talent then," Frank said and smiled. "But to answer your question… I'm not killing anyone."

"Then what are you doing here? It isn't because you're enjoying the view. You do that at the bar with a few beers." Cinnamon shook her head. "Something's up and you need to tell me."

Frank knew it was dangerous to tell her anything concrete. She had a reputation as a gossiper. He knew from firsthand experience because she'd tell him all the latest rumors and who was sleeping with who, or which girl was on the rag, anything and everything.

Cinnamon shook her head. "I get it. You don't trust me. Fine." She stood up. "I have a customer anyway. I guess I'll just make something up. The reason you're acting weird tonight. I have a vivid imagination. I'll figure it out."

"Wait…" Frank groaned. "Get me another beer and I'll tell you."

Cinnamon raised an eyebrow. "You get one free beer, Frank."

"Then buy me one." He held up the empty. "Didn't you tell me this one was on you?"

"Figure of speech. Fine. I'll be back." Cinnamon walked back to the bar and Frank watched her ass move.

She was busy with a few new rowdy idiots who wanted to get loud, get drunk and strike out with the dancers.

Frank had to piss but he didn't want to lose his table. He was thinking about taking a leak in the next beer glass she brought when he saw J.C. enter the club.

Just like Tyler thought would happen, Frank thought. *The kid is up to something. Is he dating one of the girls? Is he obsessed with one? Is he the killer? So many choices.*

None of them were any good. Dating a stripper was bad news for a cop. It put him in a bad spot. "Don't shit where you eat," Frank said under his breath. It was even worse if he was dating or obsessing about one in this club, since it was the focus on a lunatic who liked to kill pretty girls. What if J.C. was seen with one of them? Would the killer take his girl out?

Cinnamon came back twenty minutes later, after the rush and while there was a lull in the action. One of the other bartenders was covering her side.

"Now... where were we?" She smiled and sat down. "Oh, yeah, you were about to tell me you were either the killer, or you knew who it was."

"I wish it was that easy," Frank said. "I've already told you I wasn't the killer."

"You could be lying."

Frank shrugged. "You could be deflecting. Making me think I could be a suspect, when this entire time it's you."

Cinnamon grinned and nodded. "I guess we both assume it isn't the other person. Right? That would make things easier, too. I think you know something."

"I'm just trying to find clues like a needle in a haystack."

"A haystack full of drunks, strippers, gangsters, cops, beggars and thieves," Cinnamon said. She looked over her shoulder but not at the bar. "Speaking of which..."

Frank followed her eyes to J.C., who was wandering around. He wasn't drinking. He was dressed casual but his face betrayed him as a cop on the prowl for a bad guy.

Maybe I'm wrong and he's doing his job, Frank thought. *The kid is fixated on who's killing these women and that's all.*

"He's been staring at Venus for too long. What if it's a cop? That would make sense. He's got the means and he'd know if there were any clues." Cinnamon stood when the bar got crowded again. "I guess we'll know soon enough."

"What do you mean?"

Cinnamon shrugged. "If Venus is the next one dead."

Chapter Twenty-Two

Venus stepped out of the VIP room with her flustered and now broke customer. She immediately noticed two things: Frank was hiding in the corner and her would-be stalker was standing close to the entrance looking like he just walked in. J.C. looked particularly nervous, as he should be. *He really isn't too bright*, she thought. *Perfect*. Frank wasn't in here for pleasure she figured, he must be here keeping an eye on J.C.. *Even better.*

Cops obviously don't like busting other cops, but it was pretty apparent that Frank was in here to see if J.C. showed up. They must have their suspicions now. They needed something rock solid before they would make a move on one of their own. *Hmmm, speaking of rock solid.*

Venus took a long time walking toward the dorky not-too-bright rookie cop, letting him take in the whole view. She hadn't bothered to put her top back on although the management frowned upon walking around the floor topless. They wanted the girls to save it for paying customers, but Venus was well liked and had intimidated any of those who didn't find her charming. Most of the big bad macho strip club staff wouldn't say boo to her.

J.C. now looked more terrified than nervous despite his eyes being fixed on her breasts. She was just inches away when he finally found himself able to look her in the eyes.

"Hello," she said. "I don't think I've seen you here before." J.C. stayed silent but the way he was looking in her eyes told her everything she needed to know. He had been afraid that she was going to recognize him from the pool. Now that she had confirmed she hadn't, he relaxed.

"How about we go play around a little? You are so damned cute, I think I may have to give you a discount," she said, gazing into his eyes from under her enormous fake eyelashes. He still didn't utter a word as she took his hand and led him to the VIP room. He didn't even bother to order a drink.

Once back there she ordered him to take off his belt and told him to make sure he was pointed high noon. In her opinion she gave one of the best performances of her life. In fact when she felt him start to shake, she didn't let up, but let him go ahead and blast one in his pants.

"S...S...Sorry," he said. The first thing he said to her.

"It's ok, love, I wanted you to," she whispered in his ear. She did very much want him to, if only to add to the illusion. "I really like you. In fact, how'd you like to fuck my brains out? I bet a stud like you will be ready to go again soon," she said and was disgusted with herself. She never got guys off, let alone didn't charge them for it. J.C. was once again speechless. He simply stared at her. Like a dork.

"I get off in a couple of hours. How about you hang out a while then follow me home when I leave? I'll make sure the bouncers don't give you any trouble."

She knew that they were on camera back here, but no audio. This whole exchange would look totally normal to Steve or anyone else watching. Although she doubted he would be watching. Judging from his hand and his unusually strung out appearance, he had other worries. J.C.

just nodded, still staring into her eyes. She almost felt bad for him. Almost.

"Uh, ok. Here," he said, dumbstruck. Or maybe he was just always this dumb. He put on his belt, making sure the buckle hid the wet spot, and handed her a few twenties, which she accepted with a smile and a wink, despite it being much less than what he actually owed.

She gave him a little peck on the cheek before whispering in his ear. "See you later."

She left him standing by the lap dance booth as she walked back on to the floor and straight to the dressing room.

As she pushed open the door she said loudly, "Does anyone have a baby wipe? This fucking guy blew his load and I need to wipe it off my ass!"

"Ugh, here you go," said a girl named Diamond. "I fucking hate it when that happens. No warning?"

"No, he caught me off guard. I must be a little off my game tonight. Thank you," she replied. She was regarded as an OG to most of the girls. The ones who knew better held her in high regard, Queen Shit of Turd Mountain. Letting them know that she made mistakes brought a little humility and only added to the respect they had for her. She had also established that she had just had an issue with a customer who would, with any luck, get caught following her home.

She applied a fresh coat of lip gloss, body spray, grabbed a new piece of gum, and walked back on to the floor. She saw J.C. settled at the tip rail with a fresh drink. She watched him put a few dollars on the rail, but he didn't seem interested in the show. He seemed a little distant, distracted, but not by bare boobs in his face. He fell perfectly into the part she had set him up for. He looked like a lost little puppy dog waiting for his master to pat him on the head and tell him he was a good boy.

Venus walked up to the bar and asked Cinnamon for a water.

"Wow. You really did a number on that one. He looks like a zombie. I'm surprised he had any money left for a drink and the tip rail," Cinnamon said, amused.

"Yeah, he's kind of a weird one. Seems like he might just have a screw loose. Made me nervous, to be honest. I'm going to tell Jake to keep an eye on him," Venus replied.

And as soon as she saw J.C. get up to discard his used beer, she did just that. She walked up to the extra-large bald headed bouncer named Jake and told him that the dorky star-struck looking dude had been a little sketchy in the VIP. Jake was instantly concerned. He had a habit of opening the door for unruly customers with their heads. The really naughty ones got what he called the asphalt dance, which consisted of him rubbing a dude's face into the black top. The management didn't give a shit as long as it was well deserved and happened in the parking lot next door and off the Pink Pussycat's property.

"Need me to take care of him?" he asked.

"Not necessary. Just keep an eye on him. I think I may have run into him outside of here. But you know me, I always forget a face. I can never be sure if I've met someone before," she said.

She just wanted to lay the groundwork. If his face got broken before he got caught trying to follow her home, her plan may not come to fruition like she'd hoped. She slipped the big meathead a twenty before walking away. She was starting to resent the investment she was putting into all this.

She kept an eye on J.C. the rest of the night. He had just one more beer that she could tell, and that was about it. He didn't get anymore dances and when he ran out of one dollar bills, he moved back from the stage and simply watched. He seemed oblivious to Frank stalking him from the darkest corner of the room. *Really, Frank? Like no one is going to notice you sitting in the creep corner,* she thought.

About an hour before last call, Venus feigned a headache and asked to bail just a tad early. She dropped yet another extra tip for the privilege. She was going to have to throw in an extra shift at this rate. She made sure that J.C. saw her talk to the manager. He was a cop. He should be able to pick up that she was asking to leave. He was watching, and kept watching as she walked into the dressing room.

Venus walked in, packed up her stuff and Minnie walked out. She met Jake at the front door and he took her bag.

As they walked out to her car Jake said, "I saw that guy leave a few minutes ago, but he hasn't driven off yet."

"Yeah, he really freaked me out," she said in her best damsel in distress voice.

"If he tries to follow you, we'll handle it," Jake said in his best I'd really like to fuck you voice.

"Thank you so much Jake." She handed him yet another twenty. She started her car, and as she waited to pull out from the parking lot to the street, she saw headlights behind her.

Chapter Twenty-Three

Frank watched J.C. the rest of the night. Cinnamon checked in twice, letting Frank know what he already knew: the cop was not only waiting for something, but he'd gone into the VIP area with Venus and come out stinking like a dude who'd cum in his pants.

There was something going on, though, Frank knew. This was more than a simple infatuation. Was Venus fucking with the poor kid's head? She was super hot. Super sexy. Likely super manipulative. Frank knew she was nice on the surface, but she was a hustler. A predator sucking up as much cash as she could.

Frank had seen a lot of these women over the years. He'd given them a lot of money, too. He was a sucker for a good stripper sob story about mouths to feed at home, thinking it was their two children when it was their boyfriend's coke habit. Sure, they might tell you they were saving for nursing school, even though they'd dropped out six years ago to make money as a dancer and had no reason to go back.

J.C. wasn't doing anything illegal, but he was sneaking around the club where a murderer might be hiding in plain sight. It could be the DJ, who looked like a douche, or any of these meathead bouncers, who itched for a fight.

Frank got worried when he saw Venus checking out for the night and J.C. leaving within minutes of one another. Frank knew what it meant: it was time to call Tyler.

"Give me good news, Frank, or at least something I can use," Tyler said, picking up on the first ring. "I'm getting coffee but can be there in fifteen if need be."

"Coffee and a donut?" Frank asked. "I think you have a big problem."

"How big?" Tyler was immediately all business on the phone. "You think you have info about the killer?"

Frank chuckled. "Worse than someone killing strippers. Your boy, J.C., is stalking a dancer. She just left the parking lot and he's following. I'm not sure she notices him back there, though."

"What are you doing?" Tyler asked.

"Walking outside. I'm not going to run after them. My legs are too weak. This is on you now, buddy. I did what you wanted me to do," Frank said.

"No, you didn't. I need you to help me collect intel so I can catch a serial killer."

Frank laughed. "Now we have a serial killer. Nice. I thought it was just a dude who hated strippers because mommy didn't hug him. Good luck. I'm heading home. It's almost closing time, I'm hungry, and coffee and a donut sounds really good right now."

"I need to call J.C. and get him off her tail before he really screws up," Tyler said. There was a pause on the line. "Thanks, Frank. I owe you one."

"You keep piling on the I.O.U.'s and I'm gonna have to collect at some point." Frank hung up and took a walk down the street, looking for coffee and a donut before heading home.

***

The phone call could not have come at a worse time, and J.C. knew he had to answer it. He might not have been a cop for long, but he knew if Tyler was calling it was for a big reason. Maybe they'd had a break in the case?

He answered, trying to act casual. "Hey, Tyler… what's the good word?"

"Where are you right now?" Tyler seemed annoyed.

J.C. decided a partial truth would be enough. He read off the cross streets as he drove, staying close to Venus. He knew they were only a few blocks from her place.

"I want to go over a few things with you about the case," Tyler said. "Meet me back at the station."

"Now?" J.C. blurted.

"Why… where are you headed this time of night? I figured you'd be sleeping."

"I couldn't sleep so I went out for a bit."

"Where?"

J.C. felt his pulse racing. He didn't need this shit now. "I got a drink. Met a woman. Kinda busy."

"Is she in the car with you?" Tyler asked.

"No." J.C. glanced in his rearview mirror. Tyler had said it like he already knew the answer. Was he following? Had he been spying? "Is this really important? No way it can wait until morning? I think this one is going to be pretty easy." He made sure to laugh, hoping Tyler would back off.

"We're on a major case for Las Vegas," Tyler said. "No time for easy drunk chicks in a bar, I'm afraid. Tell her you'll see her another night. Until this is finished, we're going to be on a tight leash. The Captain wants us to update him in a few hours. I hope you have a set of clothes in your car because we're living at the station and in our cars. You and me, buddy. Joined at the hip."

J.C. wanted to scream. "This sounds so much better than banging a hot drunk woman. I'll see you in twenty minutes."

"I'll be waiting. Don't be late. I'm picking up coffee for us, too." Tyler hung up.

They were still a couple of blocks from her place, but he needed to peel off. He flashed his high beams at her, glad the streets weren't as full as they'd normally be.

She pulled her car over on the street, in front of an open pawn shop.

J.C. pulled up behind her and tried to casually hide his face as he approached her car. He knew the pawn shop would have cameras on the door and the street. Everywhere you went in this town cameras were watching.

He groaned inside when she stepped out. Now they'd be filmed together. This had been such a mistake. The lap dance should've been enough. He'd gotten off and had a nice memory for the spank bank. Now he was putting himself in a precarious position. He'd blatantly lied to Tyler. What if he found out? It would look really bad for J.C. not only hanging out at the strip club but following a dancer home.

"What's the matter, hun?" Venus asked. She walked over to the sidewalk and stood in front of the pawn shop. "Cold feet or you need a bite to eat before dessert?" She laughed at her own joke, not waiting for his answer, turning to look in the window of the store.

Now you're definitely in the camera eye, J.C. thought. He stayed near his car and turned his head, as if he wasn't talking to her. Just hanging out on a random street in the middle of the night, all while supposedly rushing to get to work.

"I got called into work. Can I get a rain-check?" J.C. asked.

She snapped her head around and for a second he thought she was going to go off on him. Instead, she smiled brightly. "Of course. Duty calls. You know where I work. I'm there most nights."

J.C. gave her a wave, but she laughed and rushed over, giving him a big hug. Her tits rubbed against him and he felt his dick get hard again.

She playfully looked down and laughed. "Next time, buddy."

J.C. watched her drive away and sighed. *What are you doing? This is a nightmare*, he thought. He headed to the police station, hoping his blue balls weren't going to be a distraction.

Chapter Twenty-Four

*F*uck, *fuck, fuck.* Minnie didn't want him to make it all the way back to her house, but she had been hoping that Jake would've called the police when he saw J.C. follow her out of the parking lot. It was the police that had made him divert, but not quite the way she had wanted. Maybe she didn't tip the big meathead enough, greedy bastard.

In her line of work both professional and extra-curricular being prepared for the unexpected was imperative. Minnie was disappointed that things didn't work out exactly as she had hoped. She was starting to fear that she could fall under suspicion for the murders. Cinnamon's comment about the killer being a woman had her rattled. Granted the likelihood that any one took her seriously was slight, but still troublesome. It would really only take one interested party, either the police or the guys back east for all this to go south. She was far more concerned about the latter than the former however. She knew that most cops were at least a little dirty and that meant they could be bought or manipulated. The other guys though, they were already dirty, and had no qualms about getting dirtier. If she fucked up, she would end up rotting next to Jimmy Hoffa.

After getting back to her apartment and washing the saliva from her tits and smoke from her hair, she sat on her sofa stroking her evil kitty and going back over the evidence she had left of J.C.'s guilt. If forensics got involved finding Sapphire's glitter, hair, and blood wouldn't be that hard. The blood on his door handle would leave a trace even if he rubbed the visible bit off. Hair can be pretty easy to get noticed as well. And glitter? Forget diamonds, that shit is forever.

Then there are the multiple videos. J.C. was almost certainly on tape getting lap dances from both her and Sapphire, the tricky part would be to get the owners to give them up. It could require a warrant or a subpoena if they wanted to be dicks, but they were probably ready to put this shit behind them. Maybe even capitalize on the publicity. Plus she had told multiple people that she had some trouble with him, including every other stripper who happened to be in the dressing room when she asked for a baby wipe. That was highly unusual for a girl of Venus' caliber to ask for. Only newbies and hookers ended up with cum on them. They would be all too willing to talk about that, especially if it got them attention. You can always count on an attention whore to run their mouth.

That brought her back around to Cinnamon. She was becoming a problem. Minnie had grown tired of Vegas, was ready to move on, but she needed to have all this buttoned up before she skipped town. Cinnamon might need to go. Minnie wasn't sure, but she thought that Cinnamon might actually suspect her. If she took her out now she would have to connect it back to J.C. or make it look like a suicide or accident. Things had really gotten complicated. *Probably shouldn't have killed Sass.* She pushed the invasive thought away, she had already settled that.

She figured she had two options. She could wait for the cops to do their fucking jobs and arrest J.C., or maybe she could put the other guys on his trail? She pictured Steve and his fucked up hand. She didn't think he'd got it caught in a car door. Nope, that had all the marks of the real management. He looked in a bad way, not just the bandage, but he looked like he was on something. He looked frightened. He might be receptive to her if she went to him with the information that a customer had tried following her home. That was it. The next night she went in she would tell him how scared she was that this weirdo had tried to follow her home. It wouldn't take more than that for him to make the call.

Jeff was pretending to enjoy her petting him, and got up to give her a head boop. If only to solidify the illusion that he actually liked her. She got up and fed the horrid thing before finally crawling into bed. The sun had come up while she was securing poor J.C.'s fate.

It was late afternoon when she woke. After feeding her insatiable pussycat, she ate and got ready for work. Steve would be at the club early today, and she wanted to get there before he got distracted with yet another new girl too stupid to know not to suck his dick. She went straight to his office bypassing the dressing room when she got to work. She took just a moment to un-gain her composure before she knocked on the door. He opened the door in a huff.

"Steve, can I talk to you?" she said adding a slight quiver to her voice. He would love seeing her like this. She knew she intimidated him, and seeing her even just a little vulnerable would make him feel like he had the upper hand. He motioned for her to come into his office. She took the seat opposite his desk.

"Yeah, what is it?" he asked, not unkindly.

"Last night a customer tried to follow me home, and I'm not sure but I think I saw him get dances from Sapphire.

He was really weird and scared me a little." She knew that they had probably been seen on camera in front of the pawn shop so she made sure to mention it.

"I pulled over to see if he would pass and he didn't. I told him I was going to call the police and he drove away." She stammered a little in her telling of the lie. Sometimes she wondered if she had missed her calling as an actress.

Steve's eyes got quite large and he made an inadvertent move to scratch his head before remembering the gargantuan bandage on his hand, and put it back down at his side. *Is he missing a finger or two?*

"Ok, we'll keep an eye out. Would you remember him if you saw him again?" he asked, somehow managing to not sound like a total douchebag.

"Yeah, I danced for him last night. He looks like a total dork. Cinnamon saw him and I told Jake about it." She wondered if she was getting Jake in trouble because he should have called somebody when he saw a guy follow her, but fuck him.

"Alright, go get ready. We need you tonight. The list is going to be short again," he said and then ushered her out the door.

She was almost positive that he would be taking a look at the video from the night before. It shouldn't be hard to identify J.C. on the tape, his behavior was quite odd, and he left right after she did. It was probably too dark to catch his plate on the parking lot camera, but Minnie was fairly certain Steve would recognize him as one of the cops that had been asking questions after Sass was found. She couldn't imagine a scenario where he wouldn't call his bosses. Sure taking out a cop wasn't ideal, but if anyone had the balls to do it, it was the guys back east.

Venus stepped out of the dressing room and onto the floor. It looked like Steve was still in his office. A good sign. Her revenue had taken a bit of a hit in dealing with all this drama and she was ready to empty some wallets. There really were a lot less dancers than usual, that would change as soon as the "killer" was caught. Less dancers meant more money for her. She didn't think any of the girls would be sorry or surprised to find out it was a cop. Strippers tended to be a bit on the fringe of society and had a natural distrust of cops. It could be the fact that they didn't seem to try too hard when one of them went missing or was found dead.

Venus decided to put the whole mess out of her mind for a while. She set her sights on a nicely dressed blurry eyed gentleman who looked like he might be having marital troubles. She would help him forget those troubles for a bit, good Samaritan that she was. She walked into the VIP just in time to see Steve come out of his office. He looked even more frightened than he had before. He had made the call.

Chapter Twenty-Five

Frank knew his night was going to get worse when his phone rang. It was Tyler, who was waiting outside on the street. They needed to talk.

"I waited around all day," Frank said, getting into the car. He was still half-asleep. "I'm hungry."

Tyler had a grease-stained fast food restaurant bag he handed to Frank.

"What… no buying a guy an expensive dinner before you expect me to jerk you off?" Frank laughed. "Any chance you have coffee?"

Tyler groaned. "Let's go for a ride then. We have a lot to go over."

Frank ate the food quickly and tossed the empty bag out the window.

"Littering? With a cop in the car?" Tyler shook his head. "Some things never change."

"Nope. Tell me what happened last night," Frank said. "I actually stayed awake for a few hours, staring out the window, waiting for you to call. Rolled out of bed and saw you hadn't called yet, either. Assumed you either caught your man or you went in another direction."

Tyler laughed. "Caught my man? As in… J.C. is our killer and you're asking if I arrested him. Is that it?"

Frank pointed. "Coffee. I like that place."

"I'm doing the drive thru. And before you ask… no, I don't want to be seen with you. How's that for brutally honest?" Tyler ordered two coffees without asking Frank what he wanted. After the years they'd been partners, they knew all the answers for food and drink like it was second nature.

Frank took a sip and sighed. "Now I can think."

"Now we can talk," Tyler said. "I want your opinion about J.C. Do you think he's our man?"

Frank shook his head. "I thought about it all night. My gut tells me he's an asshole. Trying to stick his dick in a place it doesn't belong. He's making bad decisions right now, using the wrong head. But a serial killer? That guy?" Frank shook his head again. "He's just an idiot."

"I agree, which is why I didn't tell anyone else about it. We spent the night working together, barely saying a word. Going over files. Boring stuff you always hated. File after file on convicted killers who might be out of prison or cold cases dating back twenty years. Paperwork. Busy work. I wanted to see what his demeanor was."

"And?"

Tyler shrugged. "Quiet. He was working to find the killer in the sheets of paper and in the computer. I didn't see him shying away from any theory, even when I hit him with a big one: it could be a cop. He seemed to think about it and agreed, but I didn't see fear or hesitation on his part."

Frank sipped his coffee. "Do you think he's a good actor?"

"Not that good."

"He would have fooled you about what he was doing if you hadn't already known the truth," Frank reminded Tyler. "He might be smarter than you think. I give it a ninety-nine point nine percent chance he isn't our man, but there's always a slim chance. Keep your eye on him."

"I intend to," Tyler said. "I left him doing more paperwork tonight. Told him I had to see a C.I. I've known for years. See what they knew."

"Now I'm a confidential idiot to you? Thanks." Frank grinned. As much as he wanted to deny it, he was having fun back on the streets, darkness surrounding him, a mystery to solve. "This is some stripper noir shit."

They both laughed.

"What do we do now?" Frank asked.

Tyler pursed his lips. "I guess we keep an eye on everything. The club. The dancers. J.C. and anyone new we haven't looked at."

Frank put out a hand. "Thanks for the burger and fries and this coffee, but you know the routine. I'm a C.I. and I need to get some walking around money."

"Seriously?" Tyler stopped at the next red light and took out his wallet. "You know the routine all too well."

"So do you. You'll get reimbursed for the ninety bucks, too." Anything over that needed to be approved ahead of time for confidential informants.

"Ninety? No way." Tyler handed over three twenty dollar bills. "That's enough for now. Bring me some actual information and we'll talk."

"I sat on your man all night and didn't even get drunk," Frank said. "That definitely calls for more than sixty bucks."

Tyler gave him another twenty and put his wallet away as the light turned green.

"You need me to go to the club tonight? It's already late."

Tyler shook his head. "Tomorrow. Go back to your normal routine for the rest of the week."

"Then I should've been at my favorite spot at the bar tonight."

Tyler chuckled. "Tomorrow. I'll keep in touch."

"Next time I want something more filling than a gut rot burger, too. Casino buffet."

Frank was dropped off in front of his building and got halfway to the door when his phone rang. He frowned when he saw it was an unknown number. Never good.

"Yeah?"

It was Gus Santonelli and he didn't sound too thrilled. "Where are you? My boys were at your apartment this evening. Steve said you weren't at the club. Don't tell me you have a life."

"No life for me," Frank said. "I took a walk. I needed to think about our situation. Get some fresh air." He looked around. If his boys were still hanging around, they would've seen him get out of Tyler's unmarked cop car. Easy enough to know who he was with.

"Did it help?" Santonelli asked.

"It got my legs moving and my head clear, I guess. You needed to talk to me?"

"I need to see you," Gus said. "Are you hungry?"

Frank smiled. "I can always eat. Are you coming to pick me up?"

"Not tonight. I have some business I need to attend to first. I'm flying in first thing. Tomorrow night we'll meet and you can tell me what you've been doing. Who you've been dealing with. What information you might have for me."

"I understand." Frank thought, if Gus the Animal was going to whack him, he'd simply send his goons to do the hit tonight.

"And, Frank…"

"Yes, sir?"

"I need you to tell me everything you know about J.C., the cop your old partner has on his leash. I think we have our first, solid suspect." Santonelli sighed. "If that's the case, we handle this guy ourselves. See you tomorrow. Good night."

Chapter Twenty-Six

Minnie sat staring at her screen with no idea what to type into the search bar. All the recent drama was starting to wear on her mind and she was ready to find a new place to set up shop. Vegas had turned out to be much messier than any of the previous cities she had worked in. This was the last place she had suspected that they would take the murders of strippers and clandestine hookers so seriously, let alone connect them. She knew that no one was looking at her, but still felt a little uneasy. Really, it was Cinnamon's comment the other night that threw her. Never before had anyone even suggested in passing that it could be a woman that might be murdering working girls.

Boston, Chicago, LA, girls go missing and turn up dead and life goes on. Her targets were almost never missed by anyone and had always been assumed to have been killed by a man. Things were much different here. Somehow this whole thing had gotten quite complicated. On the verge of becoming a real shit-show. Although she felt fairly confident that J.C. would be swept up by one faction or another, things had never been this hard.

Before pulling up her search engine with the intention of looking for a new home and hunting ground, she had taken a moment to see if she could get a sense of where the cops were in all this. It didn't look like they were considering J.C. a viable suspect. As frustrating as that was, she was confident that her contingency plan with the guys back east would end the whole debacle easily. If J.C. turned up dead, it may be easier for the cops to place the blame on him. As opposed to arresting one of their own. They could play it off as a rogue rookie cop mixed up in some nasty shit, wrap up the murders and get back to not giving a fuck.

Still, it was enough to make her feel off her game. Coupled with the fact that she had somehow blocked out killing Sass, she needed a fresh start. *Fuck it.* She typed in Miami and was instantly rewarded with a ton of links about the city. *Nope, not with my pale skin.* She wouldn't be caught dead with a spray tan. *Canada, maybe?* She would have to do some real research on that one, lots of really nice people in Canada. Damn people were always apologizing, it might be hard finding assholes to kill.

She was just about to click the link about the strip clubs in Canada when her phone rang. A flowery box of Summer's Eve came up on her screen along with the name "Steve." *Dammit.* He was calling to ask her to come in on her night off, and she knew she would have to say yes. She hit the accept button.

"Hello?" she tried to sound jovial, but was afraid her irritation was coming through anyway.

"Hey Baby." He was also trying to sound upbeat. If she wasn't so concerned with all the bullshit going on, she would've told him to go fuck himself. She was nobody's baby.

"We really need you tonight. I know it's your night off, but with all the shit going down we are really short. I'll give you a free stage fee tonight, plus two more if you would come in," he said, a slight note of desperation creeping into his voice.

"Three nights in a row is a lot Steve." She was going to go in, but was not going to let him off that easy. If she had wanted to work more than 20 or 30 hours a week, she'd have gotten a real job.

"I really need to rest and I am supposed to visit my mom tomorrow. She's been sick." Her mother had died years ago, and her father had come tumbling shortly after, but Steve didn't know that.

"Fuck. Venus, how about a whole month of free stage? You're our best girl and most reliable." *Go on,* she thought. "Please come in. My boss is going to be pissed at me for giving you a month of fees, but he'll kill me if I can't get enough girls in here to keep the guys buying drinks." He was starting to whine, and she was loving it. And he was not exaggerating in the slightest, they might really kill him.

"Ok, Steve. I'll be in a little later though, but before it starts getting busy," she said in a very sweet tone. One she actually meant this time. His whining had gratified her and made her maybe just a tad sympathetic.

"Thank you so much! You're a lifesaver," he said and disconnected.

Well fuck. She looked over to the sofa where Jeff was curled up, not giving a fuck about anything at all. She decided Canada would have to wait. Seemed much too nice a place anyway. She made a mental note to check out New York or maybe Portland. *Lots of assholes there I bet.* She stripped off what little she was wearing and made her way to the shower. She had been planning a quiet evening with some take out and a horror novel, maybe a bubble bath. She would need some time to shift back into stripper mode. *Dammit Steve.*

She pulled into the parking lot of the Pink Pussycat about an hour later than her usual time. The floor was full of drunk dudes looking for any reason at all not to go home to their wives. Week nights were mostly for the locals and traveling business men. As this wasn't her normal night, she couldn't count on any regulars. She never took or gave out any contact information like some of the other girls did, so if a customer wanted to see her they had to come on her regular shifts. It would mean a little extra work, but she might hit a big one. A lobbyist with an expense account would be nice. Weeknights meant a little extra schmoozing, but they could pay off big.

As Minnie walked into the dressing room, she noticed Cinnamon watching her. No big deal, it was a little odd that she was here on her night off. She would stop by the bar before hitting the floor to see what was going on with the rumor mill. The dressing room was nearly empty and frigid. Steve had cranked the air conditioner to near freezing to keep the girls from hanging out in there. An almost universal tactic of strip club managers. This was a little ridiculous though, she could almost see her breath and her nipples could cut glass.

Venus stepped out onto the floor and checked in with Mike the DJ. She reminded him that she liked her music like she liked her men, hard and mean. She couldn't see him blush in the low lighting, but he squirmed a bit in his too tight jeans. Her playlist would definitely be on point tonight. He could save the Whitesnake and Def Leppard for the lap dance specials. Next stop would be to get a bottle of water at the bar and to see what Cinnamon might be yammering on about tonight.

"Hi, Love! Water please," she said to Cinnamon.

"Nice to see you, Steve must have called you in," she replied.

"Yup, short on girls again," Venus said, baiting the blabbermouth.

"I heard they think it might be a customer," she said, taking the bait. "But I don't think so. Don't tell anyone, but I think it is one of the girls." She lowered her voice to just above a whisper. "The cops and management think it's some dude, but you know, a girl working here would know all the girls who got killed. I really think that's who it is." She sounded like she considered herself to be quite the slutty Sherlock Holmes.

"Oh really? That sounds pretty far-fetched. You got anything to back it up?" Venus asked. Cinnamon was used to people blowing her off, she would notice if Venus was actually interested. And she was interested.

"Between me and you..." now her voice got really low and Venus had to lean in. "I don't know which girl it was, but the night that Sass was killed I think she left with another dancer."

"Wow, did you tell anyone?" Venus was alarmed, but didn't let it show. Cinnamon had just sealed her fucking fate, and had no clue. Some girls were just hopelessly stupid.

"No, but I think if they don't come up with someone soon, I might talk to Steve and see if he will pass it on to the owners. Maybe I'm wrong, but business won't get any better until someone goes down for this shit. My tips are starting to suffer. Frank even suggested I should dance." She was pretending to have been offended, but Venus knew she had actually been flattered. Frank wouldn't have made that comment if he'd have seen the wicked C-Section scar Cinnamon took great pains to hide.

"Well, definitely business won't get better until this shit is over." Now she sounded dismissive. The last thing she was going to do was give Cinnamon the impression that she took her seriously. The poor thing had no clue just how serious it was going to get for her if J.C. didn't get taken out soon one way or another and blamed for the murders.

"Well, I got to get to work. Talk to you later," Venus walked away from the bar. Her stomach was fluttering, but her outward demeanor oozed confidence. She might just burn this whole fucking place to the ground. This was getting out of hand and quickly. Nothing pissed her off like feeling out of control and that was exactly how she felt at the moment. She stood and watched over the weeknight crowd giving the impression that she was picking out her first mark of the night. She was considering how she would in fact burn this place down along with everyone in it. She didn't think it would be that hard, the owners would collect the insurance and find another place to clean their money. And she could get the fuck out of this neon colored shithole.

As she pondered adding arson to her repertoire, she saw the owners from back east walk through the door.

Chapter Twenty-Seven

Steve had laid out a feast in his office for his boss: a plate of bar pies (that's what Gus called a slice of pizza back east, Steve was told), a tray of baked ziti and cold beer on ice.

Santonelli had only one of his boys with him, a bruiser they called Moody. Steve didn't know if it was a last name, a first name, or because of the moody look on his battered face. He wasn't going to ask. The goon had been a back alley fighter in Philly if the rumors were true. He was certainly big enough, and his knuckles were scraped and weathered from years of hitting something.

"I saw Frank out there, in the corner," Santonelli said. "Go fetch."

Steve nodded and ran out, trying to remain calm. He knew this was going to be an important night for him. He needed to give as much info as he could about anyone he was asked about, any customer, any cop, anyone. It was going to be a long night and Steve had already taken the edge off with a couple of hits. He hoped it was going to be enough.

Frank stood when Steve walked over and waved his hand.

"I need another beer," Frank said. "On you."

Steve shook his head. "I got bottles in the back. Not watered down, either. The good stuff."

Frank narrowed his eyes. "Like what? Michelob Light?"

Steve was getting a headache already. The pounding music shook him to the core tonight. He'd rather be anywhere else. The sight of dancers in thongs parading around under the flashing neon lights usually got him hard, but right now he'd trade it all in for a quiet evening in bed with his phone looking at porn. "Like, beer, Frank. Gus is waiting."

"I saw him come in. Relax. I'm busting your balls. Lighten up," Frank said and fell behind Steve, who led the way back to the office.

Steve caught the eye of both Cinnamon and Venus, both staring. He tried to smile but failed. His hands were sweaty, especially the good one.

If this somehow gets screwed up, I might lose another finger or worse, Steve thought.

"What's this shit?" Santonelli asked, waving at the food. "I'm not eating this. Steve, order me the best Italian in town and have it delivered."

"Right away, Mister Santonelli." Steve made sure not to sit behind his desk. That spot was reserved for his boss as long as he was in town. He fumbled with his phone and his mind went blank. Who should he call? What was the best Italian food in Vegas? What was food?

Frank saved his ass. "Call Milano's. They're the best." When Steve nodded dumbly, licking his dry lips, Frank took the phone. "I'll do it. You don't look so good. Maybe take a seat."

Moody laughed, a harsh sound.

Gus Santonelli sat down behind the desk and folded his hands. "Hurry up. I'm starving."

While Frank went to the corner to order, Steve sat down and tried again to smile. He was shaking.

"So?" Gus asked, putting his hands up. "I hope for your sake you did some research. Figured out what's been going on right under your big nose." He grinned. "I'd hate to have to cut that off, too."

Steve sighed in relief. When Santonelli had called to tell Steve he was on the way for a sit-down, and who it involved, Steve got to work. Well, he had Mike the DJ get to work. The camera system was beyond Steve.

"I have every time that cop shows up in the club on this," Steve said, picking up a thumb-drive from his recently cleaned desk. "He only started showing up when the girls started to get offed. Coincidence? I think not."

Frank chuckled. "He's a cop. Assigned to the murders. He started coming around because of that. Isn't it obvious? I think he got the itch for one of your girls and kept coming back to scratch it. He might be a stalker. Definitely over the line as a cop... but he's not the killer."

Santonelli frowned. "It seems like you know more than Steve does."

Steve tried to swallow but it caught in his dry throat.

"I happened to be watching when he followed the dancer outside," Frank said. "Venus."

"The one who passed along the message? Interesting." Gus pointed at Steve. "Is she working tonight?"

"Yes," Steve said triumphantly. "You want to talk to her?"

"No. I want to watch her dance and hand her a fiver for being so good at it."

Steve nodded.

Gus slammed his hands on the desk. "Go get her, you idiot."

"Right. Of course." Steve ran back out, looking around for her. At first he didn't see Venus on the stage, near the bar or wandering the floor looking for a mark.

Cinnamon was staring at him. "Have you seen Venus?"

"Yeah, she's with a big spender in the VIP lounge," Cinnamon said. Her eyes went wide. "Why... is she in trouble? Is that why the boss is here?"

Steve ignored her and ran through the curtains. Lucky for him, she was just finishing up and coming down the hall. "Hurry. Mister Santonelli wants to see you."

"Me? For what?" Venus kept walking. "I need to clean up this slobber on my tits."

"No time for that," Steve said. "Please hurry."

"I'm not going to see the boss looking like a dog drooled on me, which is exactly what happened." She seemed to be amused by her joke.

Steve grabbed her by the hand and started leading her away.

"You owe me. I was about to grab another customer," Venus said. "That's fifty bucks down the drain."

"I'll pay you," Steve said. "I'll even tip. Just hurry."

They went into the office. Frank was in the corner, looking relaxed. Santonelli didn't look too relaxed, though.

"Where's my food?" The boss was annoyed the food hadn't arrived yet, even though it had only been ten minutes or so. "Is this her?"

"I'm Venus."

"Tell me about the cop," Santonelli said. He had the thumb-drive in hand. "I've watched the club video but I want to hear what happened in your own words."

Steve knew he hadn't watched anything. He was bluffing. Moving this along quickly. He wanted to get to the bottom of whatever had happened.

"This guy's been creeping me out. Always showing up when I'm working. It's not like the regular creep, either.

He's… odd. Intense. He watches my every move," Venus said. "I tried to be nice. Give him the benefit of the doubt. He begged for a lap dance so I gave it to him. I thought that would be enough. It wasn't." She put her head down. Steve thought she might cry. He felt awful for the poor woman. "He followed me out to the parking lot. Was right behind me when I drove away."

Santonelli put up a hand. "Did we stop walking the dancers out after a shift?"

Steve shook his head. Wait… had someone escorted Venus out?

"Yes. All the time," Venus said. "Steve is a good boss."

"Who escorted you?"

Venus sighed. "Jake. He's not the sharpest pencil, to be honest, but I thought for sure he'd see what was going on and tell the guy to hang out until I was gone. It's what they're supposed to do. I hope I didn't get him in trouble."

Santonelli smiled. "No. Of course not." He turned to Steve. "Go get Jake. I need to talk to him."

By the time Steve found Jake, staring blankly at the ceiling, and returned to the office, Venus was gone. So was Frank.

"This is Jake," Steve said.

Santonelli stood and offered a hand. "Pleased to meet you, Jake. I have a few questions for you, sir."

Jake smiled and shook hands. "Sure thing, Mister Santonelli."

"So, you know who I am. Excellent. This makes it easier. If you know me you know my reputation," Santonelli said. He wasn't letting go of Jake's hand.

Steve noticed Moody pulling a pistol from his pocket and rushing at Jake.

"You messed up, Jake." Santonelli tugged on Jake's hand as Moody used the butt end of the weapon to knock Jake out, two quick strikes to the back of the head.

Santonelli smiled at Steve. "You're going to need to hire another bouncer. Maybe someone with common sense this time."

Moody lifted Jake, struggling because the men were about the same size. "I'll take him out the back and dispose of the evidence."

"Are you going to kill him?" Steve asked.

"Why… is he your boyfriend?" Santonelli laughed. "Then don't worry about him. He's old news. I'm going to be around awhile. Hiding in the shadows. Nearby. If that damn cop shows up again, you call me. Got it?"

Steve nodded. "What are you going to do with the cop?"

Santonelli watched as Jake was dragged out the back door. He turned back to Steve. "Whatever it takes to clean this mess up. My gut tells me he's our killer."

"He's also a cop."

Santonelli shrugged. "It doesn't give him the right to murder good dancers. Keep in touch."

Chapter Twenty-Eight

Venus had been annoyed at the call in, although not surprised, but now she was glad she got the call. She was now the poor little victim, the look of pity and concern on Steve's face while she described her encounters with J.C. added a thick layer of credibility to her act. She came off as the typical poor little stripper with a scary lovesick stalker. It happened all the time. She knew now that the cops weren't going to act on J.C. They either didn't think he did it, or simply didn't want to bag one of their own. Totally cool though. The other guys were now poised to handle it. She breathed a sigh of relief.

"Venus. Stand by," she heard Mike say over the speaker. That gave her about two songs before her stage. She made her way into the frigid dressing room. It was empty, the smell of cheap perfume thick in the chilly air. She made her way to her locker where she doused herself in her own cheap scent and applied yet another layer of lip gloss. She left the drool on her tits where it was. A little bonus for the next guy.

Despite the cold, she hung out until the song before her ended. She knew Cinnamon would be practically chewing her tongue off to ask her what was said in the office. The longer she waited the more desperate she would be to hear the gossip. Venus would tell her that they thought they had found the guy. It shouldn't be hard to get her off the crazy theory that a woman was committing the murders. She would make sure that Cinnamon felt like an asshole for even thinking such a thing. As if.

"Next up! Our very own red hot redheaded goddess herself, Venus!" Mike bellowed to the sparse but completely inebriated weeknight crowd. A few clapped, but most of them just sat there with utter emptiness in their eyes. Venus strutted out of the curtains and on to the stage as the intro to Pantera's "This Love" started playing. *Good boy. Follow it up with "Cemetery Gates" and this will be a good night for you.* She took a turn around the pole and took the opportunity to check out the club from this vantage point. It looks like Frank was still in the office, but Jake was missing. She felt a slight bit of remorse there. She wasn't going to be seeing that meathead again. He really should have done his job. For all he knew she could've been killed.

She slid down the pole and onto the floor just as the second song started. It was indeed "Cemetery Gates." She set her gaze on the customer waving a ten and crawled her way toward him. In her periphery, she saw Cinnamon, watching her. Waiting for her to come over and give her the dirt. The guy on the tip rail put the money between his teeth and she smashed her saliva laden boobs in his face. When she pulled away, the bill came with her, trapped between her breasts.

As she stepped off stage she lingered a bit before walking to the bar. Cinnamon vibrated with anticipation. Finally, Venus gave her what she wanted and made her way over.

"Water please," she said, completely unnecessarily, as Cinnamon already had one waiting.

"So?" Cinnamon asked with a look of a kid waiting to open her presents on Christmas morning.

"So what?" Venus asked. Teasing was kind of her thing.

"What happened in there? The boss is here, Frank went into the office, too. Steve looks scared and high. What the fuck, Venus? Tell me." She was sounding irritated.

"Well, they think they found the guy. That weirdo cop that tried to follow me home the other night. That's all I know. I'm probably pretty lucky. I think he danced with Sapphire, too. He's the one. Maybe now things will get back to normal. I mean as normal as a Vegas strip club could get," Venus said. The whole time she was talking she could see that Cinnamon was waiting for her turn to speak.

"I think they're wrong. I know they're wrong. I saw a girl leave with Sass, the night she was killed. And the other two, had pissed off at least a few other dancers. I need to go in there and tell them. What if they hurt the wrong guy?" Cinnamon was so excited she was spitting. If she insisted on covering her with even more saliva, Venus was going to ask for a fucking tip. And she just kept going.

"I found a fingernail out where Sass was found. I saved it. I bet they could match it up. Blood red. I think one of the dancers beat the shit out of her and broke her damn nail. I didn't want to say anything before, because she was fucked up so badly I figured it had to have been a man. But now I don't think so. Unique had pissed off a couple of dancers, and everyone knew that Sapphire was sucking dick in the VIP." Cinnamon was talking so fast, Venus thought her fucking tongue was going to catch fire. She took a long drink of water, buying some time for her to get a handle on her rage. She failed. Her rage would not be handled.

"That's just stupid," Venus said. "It was a dude, it was this cop. He's going to get what's coming to him and we can put all this behind us. If you go in there, you're just going to look like an asshole. An attention whore. No one will believe that bullshit. Those guys are dangerous, stay the fuck away from them."

Cinnamon looked hurt. Venus' nice girl facade had not only cracked but shattered. She had lost control, given into her rage, and she was scared. Nothing pissed her off like being afraid. If Cinnamon did have a fingernail, it wouldn't be hard to figure out where it came from. She remembered having to go to the salon the day after Sass was killed. Her nails may be acrylic, but some of her natural fingernail would be attached to it. This was all fucked.

"I'm sorry," Venus said, feigning composure. "I'm just worried about you. Really, you don't want to get involved with those guys at all. Just stay out of it. You know karma will get who is responsible eventually. Just sit back and let it happen. You know, any 'ol chick could've lost her fingernail. Who's to say they could match it to anyone anyway."

"Yeah, I guess, but I think I should at least talk to Frank about it," Cinnamon said, still butt-hurt. "I don't want some innocent guy getting hurt for something he didn't do."

"He's probably pretty caught up with the owners, why don't you sleep on it a bit? Hey, you know we've never really hung out. Maybe we should grab a spa day tomorrow. We can talk and figure out the best way to handle this." Venus knew how it had to be handled. She hadn't quite figured it out yet, but Cinnamon was going to die. And soon.

"Ok, you're probably right. I should think about it a while before I run my mouth. I have a bad habit of talking too much." *Ya think?* "A spa day sounds nice, but expensive," Cinnamon said, speaking much quieter now. "I'll call you around noon, what's your number?"

"Just give me your address, I'll come get you. My treat for the salon, too. Just promise you'll cool your jets for a minute. We'll figure this out. Sorry I got upset. I just care about you," Venus said, hoping she sounded sincere.

She stayed busy the rest of the night and was able to avoid just about everyone. She never saw the boss or Frank leave the office, but noticed Steve stalking the floor from time to time. He was the one who walked her out to her car after the club closed sometime around 3am. He didn't say a word.

When she got home, she got in the shower to wash the multiple layers of spit off of her. The anxiety didn't come off quite as easily. She lay naked on her bed. Sleep didn't come right away, but it did come. It came for Jeff, of course. The cat, who like all cats, didn't give a fuck.

Chapter Twenty-Nine

"They think it's J.C. and they'll probably go after him," Frank said, biting into another jelly donut. He wiped his mouth with the back of his hand. "Didn't you ask for napkins?"

"Glove box," Tyler said. He was staring into the darkness. "I'm not sure what to do."

"See if they can pull him off the street," Frank said. He finished his donut and reached for another on the dashboard but Tyler closed the box. "Maybe send him on vacation. I don't know. I do know, actually… if they catch him they'll kill him. They don't live by our outdated rules."

"If I get the brass involved they'll wonder why I didn't go up the chain of command sooner. I'll put myself in the line of fire." Tyler turned toward Frank. "You know how this works better than anyone. Guilt by association. My record isn't exactly exemplary thanks to you. Nothing personal."

Frank laughed. "It is personal, but I get it. This will be your second partner into bad shit. Even though I got to leave on my own two feet, there is a blemish on you. Maybe not on your actual record or in your file, but there are still too many old guard cops that remember when you and I did what we did."

"Most of them are my bosses now, too. They all kept clean and moved up, while I'm stuck where I am until I retire and they can forget about me." Tyler opened the box of donuts and took one out. Before he could close it, Frank grabbed the last one.

"Then you need to figure out what you're going to do," Frank said. "Confront J.C.? Rat him out? Keep following him and hope The Family doesn't kill him before he maybe kills another broad?" Frank shook his head. "Too many variables."

"Despite what you think, I trust your judgment when it comes to actual police work," Tyler said. "What would you do? Honestly?"

"Honestly, this isn't police work. If it was, you'd have told upper management already and put a tail on the kid. He's not experienced enough to know when he's being watched. I'd grab him off the street right away, too. These heavy hitters aren't likely to hang around and play the slots for a few days. They'll want to clean this up quickly and efficiently, and be on the next flight back to Newark."

Tyler sighed. "Then I've already put this into motion by not opening my mouth. How about your place?"

Frank shook his head. "They know where I live. They might even be watching me, but I doubt they're so good I can't see them. They show up randomly and toss me into a car."

"Why didn't you tell me before you were working with them?"

Frank put up his jelly-stained hands. "I'm not working with them. I'm taking their money and observing for them, the same as you. Working both sides for the same goal: so dancers stop dying. The money is much better on their end, by the way. Just saying."

Tyler opened the glove box and handed Frank a couple of napkins.

"Thanks," Frank said and cleaned off his fingers. "I say you get a motel outside of town. Maybe even into Henderson. Somewhere far away. Tell him you got a lead and you need to meet. Now. Before he's found and you spend the rest of the night with him on the ground, chalk-lined out."

Tyler started the car and began to drive. "I know just the place. Remember Blue Moon Motor Lodge? I'll tell him to meet me there."

Frank laughed. "I left a lot of DNA in that scuzzy place over the years. Quite a few hookers and C.I.'s high on crack offering up info and their stink boxes for a few bucks."

"You're so gross," Tyler said. He dialed his phone. It rang twice before J.C. answered. He put it on speakerphone but put a finger to his lips for Frank to keep quiet. "Hey, I got a big lead. Something huge came up, but I need you to keep it quiet. Meet me at the Blue Moon Motor Lodge as soon as you can."

"I… have a couple of errands to run, but then I'll be there," J.C. said.

"No." Tyler nearly shouted the word. "This is more important than anything you have. Got it? I'm serious. I need you to meet me. Drop everything. Make sure you're not being followed, too."

"Followed? What's this about? Should we get backup?"

Tyler sighed.

"Hurry up, kid, before something bad happens," Frank said.

Tyler shot him a dirty look.

"Who's that with you?" J.C. asked. "Your ex-partner, that dirty bastard? Seriously? Is this a setup, Tyler? We're supposed to be on the same side."

Tyler put a hand up before Frank could answer.

"We are on the same side. You're in danger. We need to get you out of Vegas. Off the grid for a few days. Trust me. This is for your own good. Where are you now?" Tyler asked.

J.C. paused. "I'm out."

"Please tell me you're nowhere near the strip club," Frank said.

"What's going on? Tell me now." J.C.'s voice cracked. "I didn't do anything to her. I swear. It was a mistake."

"What was?" Tyler asked.

"I gotta go." J.C. hung up.

"Dammit." Tyler tried calling back but it went to voicemail. "Seriously, meet us where I said. This is important. You're in way over your head. I can protect you. Just be honest with me and we'll walk it through. Call me back or meet me. Please."

When Tyler hung up he saw Frank staring at him.

"What?" Tyler finally asked. He realized he was speeding and driving recklessly and took his lead foot off the gas.

"*I didn't do anything to her. I swear. It was a mistake*," Frank said. "What do you think it means? Are we wrong? Is J.C. our killer? Is it possible?"

"No," Tyler said quickly.

"It was more a rhetorical question. Anything is possible, especially in Las Vegas." Frank whistled. "If he doesn't show…"

"He'll show," Tyler said, his words not convincing either of them. "He has to. The alternative is bad. Really, really bad."

Chapter Thirty

Minnie woke to the sound of screaming. Jeff was staring at her from the end of the bed, a look of genuine concern on his furry black and white face. The screams stopped when she closed her mouth. Jeff approached. Proof that he was some kind of demon, a normal cat would've been hiding under the bed. Minnie realized that he was her ride or die, he might be a dick of epic proportions for the most part, but he was hers.

While her heart swelled with love for the feline she had thought wished for only cat food and her demise, her brain buzzed with something far more unpleasant. She wasn't screaming from a nightmare, she was screaming from a memory. She had only slept a few hours, but those hours had been filled with blood and gore that didn't come from her fiction novels. It had come from the dark recesses in her mind that she had not dared to explore.

The image that she had woken to was Sass' caved in face, her bloodied hair matted to her skull. There was no doubt why the identification had been so difficult. This scene was not new, it was a repeat of the nightmare she had when at her spa retreat. What was new was the memory of what preceded the brutal beating.

Sass had asked for a ride home after her car wouldn't start. Jake walked them to Minnie's car and had gone back inside to finish closing up. They were about to get in the car when Sass turned to her. "Thank you so much! I don't know what I would've done."

"I'm more than happy to," Minnie had replied, her fist already in mid swing. Sass had spent the night dancing for one of Minnie's best customers. Actually, her very best customer. When she had finished, Minnie had been certain he would be waiting for her. She had walked up to him and asked him if he was ready for some real dances. He stuffed a twenty into her bra and waved her away. Humiliated and horrified, she wobbled on her heels and walked away. She walked up to Jake, handed him the offensive twenty and told him to make sure that Sass' car wouldn't start that evening.

She had been delighted when Sass had asked her for a ride. And then it was just gruesome. Every detail came back to her, and she winced with every remembered strike. She felt the rage rush through her as each new blow landed. She felt the delicate facial bones crack and give way under her knuckles. The attack had happened with such speed and force that Sass was rendered silent before she even hit the ground.

The vision faded and she became aware of her surroundings. Jeff had crawled into her lap and was purring furiously. *Awww, he's cuddling.* She had only a short amount of time to consider what this memory meant. Sass was not evil, she was not bad, she was just another stripper trying to get by in a fucked up world. Minnie had not done anyone a favor. Sass being removed from this life benefitted exactly no one.

Something in her mind slithered out of its hole. She felt as if her very being had become unraveled. A dark fog clouded her thoughts and she was unable to get a grip on the exact implications. She would figure that out later, but not from a fucking jail cell.

She leapt out of bed tossing Jeff to the side. She saw that it was getting close to noon. She needed to get to Cinnamon aka Cammi, and quickly. She crossed the room to her closet and unlocked her safe. Hidden behind the stacks of cash was an unmarked prescription bottle. She retrieved it and dumped five pills into her hand. She took them to her kitchen and ground them to a fine powder. She then took a vitamin capsule and dumped out the contents before refilling it with the generic Xanax powder. She hurried back to her room to throw on some clothes before running out the door to meet Cammi at her house.

On the way her stomach was sour with an unfamiliar sense of dread. She had to fight back the urge to vomit. This was not how she worked. She had known from her first novice attack that coming unprepared was a terrific way to get caught. She didn't work on the fly. She planned. She enjoyed that part. *Enjoyed*. She shuddered.

Minnie had gotten Cammi's address the night before but really didn't know what she was walking into. She didn't know if she would be home alone, where would her kids be? She didn't know if she would have to get her to take the pill by force or if she would simply swallow it, happy for the head change.

She pulled up to the small house, took a deep breath and walked up to the front door. She couldn't hear anything on the other side, and then she knocked. About thirty long seconds later, Cammi answered.

"Hi. I'm so happy you're here. I got my ex to take the kids today so we could hang out. I really needed it," Cammi said with a smile that should've broken Minnie's heart.

"Sweet. I needed it, too. Work has really been a bit of a shit-show. Can I come in for a few? Our appointment isn't for a little while. I brought some goodies too," Minnie said without a trace of malice.

"Yes, of course. Ooh, goodies," Cammi said as she stepped aside to allow Minnie to enter her home.

The house was small, but tidy. There was a little Barbie playhouse in the corner next to a shabby but clean sofa, and she could see a high chair just inside the entrance to the kitchen.

"Go get us some water and I'll show you what I brought," Minnie said as she took a seat on the sofa.

"I'm on it." Cammi smiled again and stepped into the kitchen. Minnie took the two pills she had brought with her. One a vitamin, the other a very lethal dose of Xanax. Cammi returned with the water, looking quite eager to swallow anything that Minnie gave her. Minnie held out the capsule with the Xanax and was pleased to see Cammi's eyes widen.

"What is that?" she asked, a gleam appeared in her eye. "Vicodin?"

"Better. Xanax. It makes for a lovely massage," Minnie replied, mimicking Cammi's smile.

"Perfect," Cammi said.

Minnie handed her the pill, and put her own vitamin on her tongue. She washed it down with a drink of water. Cammi did the same.

"That's going to be awesome. Hey, can I see the fingernail you have?" Minnie asked.

"Um, ok. It has a little blood on it. Pretty gross." Cammi wrinkled her nose but got up and disappeared down the hall. Minnie looked around the tiny living room. The walls were covered with pictures of Cammi's kid's. It looked like she had three. On the couch was a pale-yellow throw pillow which read 'Live, Laugh, Love.' Minnie wrinkled her nose.

Cammi returned with a small plastic baggie that did indeed contain a red polished broken acrylic fingernail. It was in fact, pretty gross.

"Wow, that's crazy. Have you told anyone about it?" Minnie asked, hoping the pill wouldn't take too long to take effect.

"No, I was kinda scared, and I didn't want to be wrong," Cammi said.

"That's probably for the best. Maybe after our treatments we can figure out what to do with it?" Minnie was really just making conversation at this point. Her stomach had settled down when Cammi greedily swallowed the pill. She really didn't want to have to force it. Now all she had to do was wait for her to go to sleep. One more problem solved.

It didn't take too long for Cammi's eyes to glaze over and her eyelids to grow heavy. Maybe only a half hour or so. She didn't say anything, just closed her eyes and slumped over as Minnie recited some asinine story. She had already secreted her broken fingernail in her pocket to be destroyed later.

Minnie watched as Cammi's last breath left her fatally loose lips.

Chapter Thirty-One

When J.C. didn't show up, Tyler decided to leave Frank at the room with instructions to call as soon as his partner showed up. He didn't think this was a good sign at all.

Tyler also knew he was going to get screwed in all this.

He had two options, neither of them good: have a sit-down with the brass and let them know what's been happening and try to talk his way out of getting fired… or keep them in the dark and hope he could fix this out of control mess before someone else gets killed.

If J.C. had met with me and Frank, we could've figured this out, Tyler thought. *It looks like he's our killer, even though my gut says no. Even though evidence might say no.*

It was getting late. By five Tyler would need to check in and update them on what was happening and what new leads, if any, he had.

I have shit. Not only do I have less than nothing to report, but it seems my partner might be the killer, and… oh, yeah, I've known for awhile but didn't want to tell you because my main C.I. is my other former partner, you remember Frank Michi? Yeah, the guy you fired for a lot of bad things, most you couldn't prove, but you know he's crooked and some of that stained my jacket too, but hey, he's my main source and I've been feeding him cash to sit in a strip club and get drunk and now The Family from back east is involved and... fuck. Tyler pulled into a drug store lot and punched the steering wheel in frustration.

He was a good cop. Hell, he was a great detective. He'd been in worse spots than this. At least he had a suspect, even if it was his partner. He had clues, too. An idea about whoever was killing the dancers.

Tyler tried to call J.C. again and left a short but angry message on his phone, making sure not to say anything that would implicate him. It was more along the lines of *answer the damn phone, partner, we've got work to do.*

He was about to pull back onto the road when his phone rang. It was Frank.

Tyler sighed in relief. "Is he there?"

"Uh, no," Frank said. "But Santonelli wants to see me. Right away. He also wants me to give him everything I have on J.C. because he's convinced that's the killer."

"He'd risk everything to kill a cop? Is he nuts?" Tyler couldn't believe this.

"Is he nuts?" Frank laughed. "Of course he is. The man is certifiable. A true old school maniac. He won't kill J.C. before he tortures him a million ways to Sunday. He'll get a confession out of him, even if it's not true. Doesn't matter. I was hoping you had J.C."

"No. Not a word from him. I'm going to go by his apartment and see if I can find anything," Tyler said. He left it unsaid he hoped not to find his body riddled with bullet holes.

"Call me when you get there and check in, but if there's anything off, get your ass out," Frank said. "Then we need to take a breath and figure things out. You follow what I'm saying?"

"Yes, I do." Tyler took a deep breath and exhaled. "Frank, I want to thank you for the help. I know you're putting your neck out for me."

"Damn straight I am," Frank said. "Now go find this asshole before the mobsters or the real killer does."

Tyler drove to J.C.'s place. He'd been there a few times but never inside. Only to pick him up a couple of times when his car was having trouble.

No one answered when Tyler knocked on the door, which was no big surprise. He looked out to the parking lot again but J.C.'s car wasn't there. He walked to the back parking lot. No car.

"Can I help you, officer?" A pale woman with crooked teeth asked from where she sat in the grass.

Tyler smiled. "Is it that obvious?" He opened his jacket and showed her his badge and weapon. "I thought I was dressed casual."

"It's a hundred degrees. The only men who wear suits in this are cops or killers." She put a hand up to block the sun. "Are you looking for the other cop?"

"Yes, ma'am."

She blew air through the large gap between her front teeth. "Ma'am? Ha. Ain't you an ass-kisser. He ain't here."

"Any idea where he went? When he left? Was he alone?"

She tried to stand and eventually got there, a smile on her face. Even her lips were crooked. "In the television shows they take out a little pad and a pencil. Lick the end of the pencil and start writing. So many questions."

Tyler was getting impatient but matched her smile, although his mouth and teeth weren't messed up. "This isn't an interrogation, ma'am. Just one cop looking for another cop. That's all."

She turned and pointed. "I live right there. My husband works on the road. From here to Reno to Los Angeles and back. Trucker. I see him on weekends if I'm lucky. Or not lucky depending on if he's been drinking. Anyway, your cop friend packed a bag of food and water bottles, put a bunch of clothes in a backpack and took both of his guns from his safe and drove off last night. About ten."

Tyler grinned. "And how do you know all of that?"

The woman pointed. "He leaves his blinds open. From my front window I can see right down into his apartment. He's a lonely man," she said and laughed. "Lots of adult videos at night. He's a big fan of strippers."

"How do you know that?" Tyler tried to remain calm.

"Most of the time he's not watching porn. It's a lot of dancers swinging around on poles and him getting lap dances. I mean, it might be him filming or it's some weird website he's watching." She smiled again. "I used to be a stripper in Reno."

Tyler thought she was more likely a hooker, but kept his mouth shut.

"Thanks for the information," Tyler said and began walking away.

"Aren't you forgetting something?"

Tyler turned back.

"Two things: you're supposed to give me one of your business cards and tell me to call you if he returns or if I remember anything else. Like in the TV shows."

Tyler sighed and took out a card, handing it to her. "The other thing?"

She pointed at J.C.'s apartment. "Whenever he came out and saw me, he took pity on me. Because my husband is on the road all the time, and when he's home he smacks me around. Doesn't let me smoke."

"And?" Tyler asked.

"And so he gives me ten bucks for smokes," she said cheerily.

Tyler turned back and walked away. "Cigarettes will kill you. This is God telling you to quit."

"Jerk," she said, but Tyler was already halfway to his vehicle.

This was going from bad to worse. J.C. might be in the wind. Was he the killer? If he was on the run, it made it look really bad for him. Videos of strippers on his TV?

Tyler stopped and went back to the apartment. If it was true, he'd need the tapes. Or the laptop the movies were on.

As if J.C. was stupid enough to leave evidence behind, Tyler thought.

Instead of kicking down the door and creating a scene, he went in search of the office. He'd flash his badge and have the super open it for him.

The woman was back on the grass and she was pointing. "Office is over that way, jerk."

Tyler stopped, took out a twenty, and tossed it on the grass next to her.

Chapter Thirty-Two

Minnie stopped at a convenience store on her way home from Cammi's to pick up a cheap burner phone. Vegas still had a few ancient payphones lurking about town, but they were too filthy for even someone who allowed strange men to slobber on her private parts to fuck with. She got back in her car and activated the phone. She wanted to eliminate any doubt that J.C. was the stripper murderer but wanted to think a moment as to where to place the call. Even a novice forensics investigator would be able to find the blood she had planted on his car. The glitter Sapphire had transferred would be sticking to anything it could. Washing machine be damned. *What happens in Vegas stays in Vegas* applies to just about everything but glitter and herpes.

She was sure the *back east boys,* as she thought of them now, were convinced, but the cops seemed utterly reluctant to seriously consider J.C. as a suspect. Cammi's death might complicate things just a tad, but her death would most likely be ruled an accidental overdose. Black market benzos were all too common, as were overdoses. Minnie couldn't fathom how it could be construed as anything other than an unfortunate coincidence. She just wasn't comfortable leaving J.C.'s fate up to a bunch of criminals. She wanted any chance of any suspicion directed her way to be eliminated, and that meant that these damn cops needed to find what they were so unwilling to look for. The question now was who to place the anonymous call to.

Should she just call the tip line? The front desk? Shit, she had the personal cell phone numbers of both Frank and his old partner Tyler. She needed to think. If she called one of them, they might wonder how their numbers were obtained. She didn't want them wondering anything like that. Tip line it was, then. She rehearsed her narrative in her head. She didn't need to say much, just enough to poke them in their lazy cop asses. She punched in the number and only had to wait a split second before a serious sounding female voice picked up on the other end.

"Las Vegas PD tip line," the voice said.

"You have a cop by the name of J.C. who has been murdering exotic dancers. I saw him leave the apartment of the victim named Bette on the night she was killed," Minnie said in a voice approaching a whisper. That should've been enough, but these cops seemed determined to avoid investigating one of their own so she decided to spell it out for them. "Check his fucking car for blood." Minnie hung up.

She started her car and drove out of the parking lot, heading towards the unsavory part of North Las Vegas. She stopped close to the skid row which boasted a rather impressive albeit pathetic row of tattered tents and makeshift shelters. The city had provided several portable toilets to mitigate the amount of human feces on the streets with only marginal results. She got out of her car, held her breath and stepped into the nearest one.

Once inside she snapped the cheap phone in half and dropped it into the depths of foulness below. Next she took out the little baggie with her fingernail in it and dropped it on the floor before crushing it with her shoe. She then emptied the contents into the yawning maw of the toilet followed by the baggie. *Good luck finding any DNA in there,* she thought and forgetting herself took a deep breath. Retching, she spilled out of the port-a-potty and got into her car. Dousing her hands in hand sanitizer before turning the key.

She should've felt more in control now, but didn't. Whatever had freed itself from the dark recesses of her brain was driving her thoughts. From early on in her life, she had felt confident in her heroics. She was secure in her motivation to help humanity by ridding it of its weak links. Every time she tried to turn her thoughts to what the memory of Sass' murder actually meant in that context, that dark thing obscured her efforts. Its unnamed malevolence simply wouldn't allow her to explore her own mind. She felt fractured, broken, unhinged. There were now two factions fighting for control of her thoughts.

She suspected this thing, this monster in her own mind, was protecting her somehow. Protecting her from what, exactly? That she was in fact just a psychopathic killer? A sick and twisted sadist that enjoyed murder? That she lacked any and all form of conscience, was it protecting her from the realization that she was the very thing she thought she was protecting the world from? Was she evil?

Her vision darkened, she felt her car start to drift with no sense of control. Suddenly the rumble strips on the highway growled her back to reality just as she was about to leave the road. Cautiously she made her way back to her apartment.

Jeff was waiting for her as she walked in. His ravenous eyes distracted her from her thoughts. She fed him and fell onto her sofa. Her mind turned inward as she closed her eyes. She recounted her many exploits in homicide. Starting with her first, she recalled each one in as much detail as she could muster. Every single one brought with it a sense of power and control. Her newly acquired dark friend that now occupied her conscious mind delighted and marveled at each one. The planning, the risk, all of it was thrilling. Exciting her to the core.

As she pictured each of her victims, she was no longer convinced that they were bad people. She had assumed that Sass had been an anomaly, an outlier. A simple flaw in her motivation. She no longer believed that at all. Her thoughts turned to the now cooling body of Cammi lying on her sofa, and the poor stupid cop that would either end up in jail for the rest of his life or picked apart by coyotes out in the Nevada desert. They had been innocent and undeserving of their respective fates along with all *well maybe not all*, of her victims. She was not the good guy, she was not the hero. She was the menace that humanity needed protecting from.

The black presence in her mind assured her that all this was good. She was still justified in her killings. Even if the justification was simply her pleasure and to preserve her freedom. Her thoughts were overcome now with this blackness, her entire sense of self upended. Her mind hadn't snapped, it had collapsed. If this was who she was, who she wanted to be, then why would she go to such lengths to convince herself otherwise? Why not simply revel in her own malevolence and embrace it? Was there some part of her that longed to be good?

A profound dissociation overtook her as she opened her eyes and rose from her couch. Jeff started to howl, but she didn't hear him. She shuffled as if in a dream to her closet. Her fingers worked without thought as she unlocked her safe. Those same unthinking fingers closed around the pill bottle and unfastened the cap. She poured the contents into her hand, six pills, more than enough.

Jeff uttered a mourning whine and frantically butted his head against her back. She pushed him away and he screeched. The monster inside her head was utterly quiet, she would save the world from herself. She could still be the hero.

Chapter Thirty-Three

Tyler was livid. "What do you mean, he called out sick? Are you kidding me?"

Sergeant Edler shrugged his shoulders and went back to eating his apple pie. "He said he wasn't feeling well. Legally, I can't ask him what's wrong. I don't want the Chief breathing down my neck for questioning an officer, especially a newbie. We have enough problems with hookers getting murdered in the streets."

"Strippers."

Edler waved his hand. "Whatever. All the same to me." He looked up, a bite of apple pie on his fork. "Forget I said that. Not really politically correct. I hate everyone equally." He shoved the pie into his mouth.

Tyler knew the sergeant was a selfish prick, who only cared about his standing in the political climate of LVPD. He was so far up the Chief's ass he knew what the man had for breakfast. "I've been trying to get in touch with him."

"He's sick," Edler said. "Don't ask and don't tell. That's my motto. He'll be back in a couple of days. He has sick time to kill, and..." The sergeant shrugged. "What he does on his own time is his prerogative."

Unless it has to do with screwing up and stalking a dancer, Tyler thought. He had no doubt J.C. was doing things he shouldn't be doing, but he knew he wasn't killing anyone.

"Is that it? Don't you have some dead women to find a killer for?" Sergeant Edler asked.

"I do." Tyler bit his lip and left the office, wanting nothing more than to punch the walls as he moved down the hallway. The man was an ass. Tyler knew he'd someday be the Chief, too. It made no sense to get on his bad side and be his punching bag while he was the big boss.

Better to keep his head down, clear some cases, and retire down the line with a full pension and his head intact.

Where had J.C. gone? He'd fled. That much was obvious. How far? There were countless motel and casino rooms he could hide in. Roads out of town in all directions. He could be anywhere.

Tyler didn't even know where the guy was from. They'd only been partners for a short time, and Tyler had had enough partners after Frank to know better than to get too friendly. He was the pariah in the department. Only the rookies got tossed with Tyler Fitt into an unmarked car. Want to move up and become a detective in Las Vegas? First you have to survive the crash course with Tyler to see if you're good enough. To see if you're as crooked as he supposedly is.

He tried calling J.C. again but didn't bother with another message. By the time he got to his car and drove out of the lot, he was calling Frank.

"No good?" Frank asked. "I asked Steve at the strip club if he was lurking around there but he's not on camera anywhere. What about the dancer he was stalking? Want me to get her number?"

"Yeah, that will work," Tyler said. "And her address. Maybe he's in his car whacking off, peeping into her damn window. I don't know. I got nothing."

"Same. I'll call you back."

Tyler didn't even know where he was driving to. He started cruising past the strip clubs, making a loop through town and trying to get his head clear. It was no use.

His phone rang but it wasn't Frank. It was dispatch on a private line.

"Tyler, there's a problem," the woman said. He couldn't remember her name off-hand. He'd only talked to her a few times. She'd been working long enough he should know it, though. *Some cop you are*, he thought bitterly. The wheels were coming off.

When he didn't respond, lost in his own thoughts, she continued. "We received an anonymous call. It was a woman. She sounded scared. I can play you the taped call."

"Go ahead." Tyler looked for a spot to pull over.

You have a cop by the name of J.C. who has been murdering exotic dancers. I saw him leave the apartment of the victim named Bette on the night she was killed. Check his fucking car for blood.

Tyler sighed. "It would help if we had his car. Having J.C. would be better. I don't recognize the voice, but she was whispering. Did we locate where it was coming from?"

"Looks like a burner phone. Got them working on it now. See if they can find something," she said.

"Why did you call me? Does the sergeant or the chief know?"

"No. I called you first," she said.

"That's not the way this works," Tyler said. "You could get in a lot of trouble if they found out you gave me a head's up before telling them."

She chuckled. "Are you going to tell them?"

"Nope. Not a chance. Can you do me a favor and give me a few hours to sort this? Is that asking too much?"

There was a pause on the line. "I get off in three hours. Maybe the calls coming in will be so intense I'll forget to mention it to the brass until I hand in my sheets. If they even bother to look at them tonight."

"Thank you very much," Tyler said. "I owe you one."

"Yes, you definitely do. I'll be taking payment with many drinks very soon."

Tyler laughed. He wondered if she was being funny or flirty. Either way he liked it. "You got it."

Still, with nowhere to go, he kept driving. He called Frank. "What are you doing?"

"I just got off the phone with Steve. It looks like the bouncer, Jake, was taken out of Vegas. Likely killed and buried in the sand. Hopefully far away."

"Hopefully." Tyler didn't want to sound callous, but a body in the desert was better than a body in an alley or in a casino. Not their immediate problem. "I'm going to pick you up."

"As long as you buy me a meal."

"You never stop eating. Fine. See you in five minutes."

Tyler headed toward Frank's apartment. The stakes had gotten higher. The Family was in town, and he'd not shared the information with his colleagues. That was a strike.

He knew Jake was dead, a potential witness to whoever was killing dancers. Strike two.

It looked like J.C. wasn't as innocent as first thought, but Tyler needed to find him before the mobsters or the cops did. Definite third strike. You're out.

His phone rang again and he groaned. This time it was dispatch on the official line.

"This is Teresa again."

Teresa. I need to write that down, Tyler thought. "Please tell me you have good news."

"When we call it's never good news. We have a potential suicide of someone connected to the strip club," she said. "Cammi Wheeler. Also known as Cinnamon. Her neighbor found her."

Tyler wanted to scream. Where the fuck was J.C. and did he have anything to do with this one, too?

Chapter Thirty-Four

The sharp sudden pain in her wrist brought her out of her stupor. Jeff's canine teeth were still embedded in her skin as he looked up at her. She closed her fist around the pills, and he finally let go. The pain was immense and beautiful. Slowly she stood up and made her way to the kitchen where she ran cold water over her wound. She opened her hand and let the pills fall into the garbage disposal.

She watched as her blood followed the Xanax, dripping dark red and turning pink as it blended with the water. She looked at her injury. Two deep puncture wounds, the damn thing barely missed her artery. To have avoided death by overdose only to bleed out would've been pretty fucking ironic. Jeff jumped up on the kitchen counter for the first time in his life, putting his hairy cat butt where she prepared food. She surprised herself when the urge to knock him down didn't come.

Using the first aid kit she had under the sink, she dressed her wound. Trying to remember the last tetanus shot she had had. She would need to watch for infection. It seemed she didn't want to die after all. The darkness in her mind seemed to have retreated for the moment. Holding her wrist, which was still oozing blood although it had slowed, she laid down on her bed. Jeff hopped up and lay next to her, putting his head on her leg.

"What the actual fuck? Asshole," she said to him with the utmost affection. He started to purr.

She closed her eyes and tried to understand what had just happened. She had never thought about killing herself, it made her feel weak. Angry. She was angry at whatever had intruded her mind and sent her down that hole. *Had it intruded though, or had it just been hiding?* That thought scared the shit out of her. Her facade had crumbled. No it had not crumbled, it fucking exploded. Did she feel guilt? Remorse for the people she had killed over the years? She wasn't even sure of the exact number. Only real sickos kept a kill count.

She probed her feelings, afraid that whatever screwed up shit had just happened to her mind wouldn't happen again. It's not like she could go talk to a professional, seemed like a sure bet that they were obligated to report multiple murders. The carefully crafted illusion of righteousness had thoroughly evaporated. The question was, how did she feel about it? The answer? Nothing. She felt nothing at all about it. People die. Everyone starts dying the day they were born. No, she felt stupid. She felt false and fake. That was fine when dealing with other people, perfect in fact. She felt stupid for buying into her own bullshit. She had fooled herself. That was fucking unacceptable. Somehow, she fell asleep.

Her phone woke her only a couple hours later, a box of Summer's Eve came up on the screen while Slayer's 'South of Heaven' played. She ignored it, and when it stopped she didn't get the voicemail notification. She knew why he was calling anyway. It was not her night to come in and she was definitely not doing him any more favors. Besides, the strip club was a bad place to be with an open wound.

It was late afternoon. She should've been wide awake. This was her morning. She felt wiped out however, drained, empty. She would call Steve back and tell him the truth. That her demonic cat had bitten her and she would need a few days off. She might need antibiotics, lucky she didn't need stitches. The club wouldn't want her there with a bloody scab either. Bad boob jobs were cool. Festering bite wounds? Not so much.

She hadn't eaten in quite a while, but food was about the last thing she wanted. She felt wounded. She wasn't quite sure how she would proceed. She thought that the murders and J.C. were not her problem anymore. What she had set in motion would play out without her help. They would find Cammi and find all the drugs in her system, could be an overdose or suicide. Either way, Minnie was certain she would be in the clear. Minnie would spend some time alone, in her apartment, with her knight in furry armor and get her fucking shit together. She didn't want to think about anything for a while.

She picked up her phone and dialed Steve's number, hoping that she got her timing right and he wouldn't answer. It went straight to voicemail. *Thank fucking God.* She really didn't want to talk to that fucker right now.

At the beep she said, "Hey Steve I saw you called. I won't be able to come in for a few days. My damn cat bit me, I swear to God, and it's really gross. Probably going to scar, too. I'll try and come in in a few days. Maybe I can find something to wear to cover it up."

She hung up and turned off her phone. She had exactly no reason to turn it on again. She would spend the next couple of days figuring out what the hell she was going to do next. If he called and she didn't answer, fuck him. There were a hundred other clubs in Vegas.

She spent the next two days doing just what she planned, nothing. Jeff was on board with this plan and beside her the whole time. She read, watched a movie or two, and took long warm baths. By the second night, she started to feel a little more put together.

Minnie was able to admit to herself that her objective had not been serving justice to those who may never face it. She knew now that her desire had been to kill pure and simple. While that scared her at first, she had come to face it. She looked at herself in the mirror and saw a killer who acted out of self preservation and pure desire. And she could live with that. She was who she was and she couldn't do a thing about her past, and didn't even want to. Perhaps the most liberating part of her realization was that she was able to accept that about herself. She wasn't going to be shouting *I'm a sociopathic serial killer. Always follow your dreams kids!* But understanding who and what she was, made her feel alive. The darkness that had retreated was back now. Revealed and exposed, it was not some intruder in her mind, it was her very essence. It was here to stay now with no reason to stay hidden. This black presence was her authentic self and damn if it didn't feel good to be bad.

When she was done with Vegas she would move on, and she would kill again. It's who she was. She hated the fact that she had been able to convince herself that she was killing to stop bad people from being bad people. It really pissed her off in fact. There was something else that was eating at her too. Innocent people were really easy to kill. She was ready for some real challenges. Minnie was far too talented to be taking on easy prey.

That's exactly what she had been doing, killing the weak, the gullible, and the stupid. That was going to end. She was going to go after the real bad guys. She wanted the game, the hunt, and she wanted the challenge, no she needed the challenge. No more pathetic strippers and street walkers, no more lovesick customers, or yappy bartenders. Nope. Minnie was going to go after the baddest of the bad, if only for the pure joy of the conquest. There was a certain appeal to the thought that she was delivering revenge. Like closing a circuit. Bad things happen to bad people.

She had come to this decision lying in a warm bubble bath which had long since started to cool. She smirked a bit as she sat up. She reached for her towel where Jeff was sleeping while depositing plenty of cat hair. He gave an annoyed little chirp as she brushed him off.

"Move fur-ball," she said. She looked down at her wrist and was relieved that there was no sign of infection. She would need to find something to cover it up though, bracelet or something. No one wanted to see a Band-Aid on a stripper.

She dried off and grabbed her darkened phone. As she switched it on she was thinking she might call in for delivery. She was ready for a big meal to celebrate her new found clarity. Her device came back online. It appeared that Steve had been trying to reach her.

Chapter Thirty-Five

The quiet before the storm, Tyler thought. Two days without a lead. No new killings. No J.C. and no mobsters making waves, either. Something was going to break, and break bad. Really, really bad.

Frank had been out and about, cycling through the strip clubs and the common spots where J.C. might be hiding. "He's gotta eat sometime, and if he's still in Vegas, he isn't going to go far," Frank had said.

It also meant Frank ate at all of those places, ostensibly to gather intel, but also because Tyler was feeding him cash for meals like it was going out of style.

Brass still hadn't put it together, and Tyler made sure to stay away, preferring his vehicle for his office.

The jury was still out on whether or not Cammi's death was suicide or murder. On one hand, maybe she was freaked out by all of the killings and wanted to go out on her own terms. Maybe she even knew who the killer was, and couldn't face them. Or her own conscience.

She might also be the next victim of the serial killer. It would make sense, too: she worked at the strip club where the deaths are occurring, she might know the killer because he's a regular customer, or it's one of The Family dirt-bags.

Tyler shook his head. The Family was looking for this guy, too. Unless one of them was a superb actor, it wouldn't be them. He knew that already.

He also didn't completely believe it was J.C., either. Tyler prayed it wasn't, and knew it was for his own selfish reasons. Another partner gone bad? He'd thought about this angle a lot lately, and he felt like shit for thinking it, but it was what it was.

Frank called just as it was getting dark. Tyler knew he needed to sleep. Go home and relax. Watch some TV and get his mind off of this case for a couple of hours.

"Steve talked to Venus and Roxxi," Frank said. "The blonde Roxxi, not the one with the fucked up unicorn rainbow stripes in her hair and on her landing strip. They're both alive and well. Just spooked or whatever. They took off a couple of days. That's all."

Tyler assumed they were both still breathing. The killer wasn't too keen on hiding a body. He wanted them found and quickly. Why? The meeting he had in about an hour would hopefully give him some answers. "So… no killings for at least forty-eight hours. More if you believe Cammi was a suicide."

"No way she killed herself," Frank said quickly. "It might not be our guy, but it's a murder. I think she knew something. Maybe not about our serial killer but about Steve or Gus Santonelli. Maybe even all the way to the top of The Family. Who knows? She was killed to shut her up."

"You're probably right." Tyler sighed. "I've called J.C. a hundred times. Nothing. I'm running out of patience and options. My bosses are going to keep asking questions, and it's only a matter of time before they wonder how that idiot Edler gave J.C. time off in the middle of a high-profile murder investigation."

"I got nothing else. I'll make the rounds again tonight. Gus left town again but his goons are still around. Harassing Steve and making the club tense. A lot of the girls are moving on. Out of Vegas. At least three of them."

"Maybe one of them is the killer and some other shitty town will have to deal with this then," Tyler said, joking. "If I can't solve this one, I'm screwed. The politicians are going to roast me over a slow fire."

Frank laughed. "Thanks for the suggestion. I'm going to try out the new barbeque joint on my way to the strip club."

Tyler hung up before Frank could ask for more cash.

He drove to the police station but parked a block away, sneaking in through the parking lot door and keeping his head down, as if he was busy thinking.

Three men, all in suits, were waiting for him in the conference room. All with hands folded over a thick folder. They stood as one and offered hands.

Tyler didn't bother remembering the FBI agent names. They all used lame fake ones like Agent Jones, Agent Smith and Agent Johnson. Those might've been the three names they used, in fact.

"We think we've put together a profile you're going to find interesting."

Tyler was tired. He nodded and hoped they weren't going to spend too much time trying to impress him, or over-explain all of it. Plus, Tyler had brought them in from the other coast on the sly, hoping no one would notice the cost of flights for the men. He'd asked for one but the FBI insisted on sending this trio.

After a long, drawn out two hour presentation, Tyler sighed and glanced at his paragraph of notes. He needed another cup of coffee but needed to get through this and then home to bed. Even a couple of uninterrupted hours would be a nice change.

"Let me see if I can sum it up, gentlemen," Tyler said.

"If you have any questions," the middle agent said, "We're here for the next two days. We'd have no problem giving this presentation to your superiors, as well."

Tyler put up a hand. "That won't be necessary. I'm the senior detective, and fully in charge of this matter."

When the trio didn't respond, Tyler tapped his pen on the sheet of paper in front of him. He knew one of the thick folders was also going to be handed over to him to study as well, although he'd managed to cut through the bullshit and get to the bottom line.

"A white male, possibly as young as thirty, who knows the ins and outs of the business. Might be a former bouncer, owner or DJ. Has definitely worked at the club where the women have been targeted. He stalks his victims. He's not prone to mistakes. The chase is part of the high, maybe even more important than the kill. While he uses different variations of the kill, he is using a pattern. He might be homosexual. Hates women. Likely mommy issues. Maybe abused as a child. Something set him off, like a recent breakup. Maybe he's married to a woman and she caught him with a dick in his mouth."

Tyler looked up and smiled as the trio looked uncomfortable. He shook the piece of paper. "This sounds like everyone from Gacy to Bundy. Hell, I've read enough about Ed Gein to know it could be him, as well."

"It's a bit more complicated than that," one of the men said.

"I'm sure it is." Tyler stood. "Gentlemen, this has been very helpful and informative," he lied. "If I need your help further I will let you know. Thank you for your help."

He showed them to the door. They'd left one of the folders on the table. He wanted to toss it in the garbage, but was afraid someone might find it. Instead, he shoved the sheet he'd written on inside and tucked it under his arm.

"Who are they?" Sergeant Edler asked, walking by in the hallway.

"Jehovah's Witnesses. Trying to recruit me," Tyler said.

Edler was staring at Tyler. "You don't strike me as a religious man."

Tyler shrugged.

"Meet me in my office in an hour. I want a debriefing on everything happening with this case. Then you need to go home and get some sleep. You look like shit."

Chapter Thirty-Six

Minnie set down her phone after talking to Steve. He sounded relieved to hear from her. Apparently he had feared she was dead. They had found Cammi, and there had been some talk that she might be yet another victim. Although Steve implied he thought it was an overdose, right before asking her to come in tonight. She had told him that she would. She did really enjoy the sound of desperation in his voice.

She took a look at her wrist, it wasn't pretty. In fact it was downright hideous, but looking like it was healing. Venus considered herself a minimalist when it came to stripper costumes. The less she wore, the quicker she was naked, the more money she made. It was just that simple. She never messed around with anything other than a bikini or even just a g-string if the club allowed. She certainly didn't own anything with sleeves.

Minnie opened the door to her closet and ignored the slight shiver that passed through her as she saw the safe. She reached up to the top shelf to a large box which contained a few stripper odds and ends. As she pulled it down, it tipped over and she suddenly found herself in a shower of g-strings, mismatched bikini tops, and she just missed being impaled by a spike heeled platform shoe. With a sigh, she began rummaging through the mess and found a set of matching leather spiked wrist cuffs. *Perfect.* She remembered getting in a tiny amount of trouble for "accidentally" jabbing a customer with these, but they would have to do.

As she walked in the club that evening, it was obvious that something was off. Well, everything really. The whole place had a dark and eerie feeling, more than usual. Behind the bar was Sunny, a sweet little Asian girl who tended the bar weekend day shifts, and a weeknight or two depending on her school schedule. One of the two or three girls who really were working their way through college. In Sunny's case, nursing school. Venus tended to like her, she was really Cinnamon's polar opposite. Quiet, thoughtful, and soft spoken, her presence made the atmosphere feel heavy with her lack of chatter.

Venus made her way to the dressing room, where the silence was even heavier. There were only three girls getting ready, and one of them was brand new. Her silence was more indicative of her new girl anxiety rather than grief. Venus saw her eyes were a little too wet. It was pretty early to be drunk, but that was her first impression. Until one of the girls went over to ask if she was ok. The tiny little squeak that came out of her said she was very much not ok, the torrent of tears that followed confirmed it.

"I don't know what to do. He said if I tried to go anywhere else, he'd make sure they wouldn't hire me," the new girl said. She had started to quiver now, and Venus was now compelled to get involved. She didn't want to look like an ass so she walked over and got close to the girl.

"What's your name?" Venus asked, and found that she did feel just a little badly for the poor thing. Something had really upset her.

"Lexi," she said.

"What's up Lexi? You're fucking up your eyeliner," Venus said, trying to lighten the mood just a tad. This wasn't the first time she'd had to chill a girl out who'd had an argument with a boyfriend.

"He told me not to say anything. I just got into town and got all my paperwork paid for, I really need to work." Now she was babbling.

"Well, it's not like any of us are huge fans of the management here. You're cool." Venus motioned to the other two girls in the dressing room. They were all huddled around the new girl now.

"The manager told me to suck his dick or go somewhere else. I got scared. The manager at the club at home never did anything like that. I didn't know what to do. I told him I couldn't. That I had a really bad canker sore, that I thought it was herpes." She was really sobbing now, but Minnie took an immediate liking to the little thing. *Huh? Herpes to get out of a forced blowjob? Smart girl.* She wasn't easily impressed, yet here she was.

"He said to fuck him before I left tonight or don't bother coming back, or go to another club. He said he'd make sure I wouldn't work in Vegas. He said this is how it works here. I spent so much to get here and on all my licenses. I don't have enough money to get home if I don't work. I don't even have enough for my hotel tonight. I don't want to fuck him, he's kinda… gross."

"No, he's not kinda gross… he's really, really gross. That's only how it works for the stupid girls, and I have a hunch you're not stupid. Clean yourself up, and get out on the floor. Stay away from Steve, and for fucks sake, don't fuck him. Come see me when your shift is over and I'll make sure you get out of here without him seeing," Venus said, masking her anger. She may not be easily impressed, but she was easily angered. Holy fuck was she ever angry.

Steve had been a douche and she knew that he took advantage of girls, but this was new. The favors he had gotten from the new girls in the past, she was pretty sure he at least paid something. She knew that the boss had fucked him up, losing a finger was pretty fucked up, and that he was going to take it out on the girls at some point. She really had thought that turning the air down to arctic temperatures would be the extent of it. She felt kind of stupid now for thinking that he would stop there. Nope, he intended to take his stress out on the girls.

Venus had really hoped that she wouldn't have to kill again before she left Vegas, and she really wanted a tougher challenge than Steve. He wasn't some criminal mastermind, just a piece of shit who really needed a long dirt nap. Venus would really enjoy getting rid of him. She wondered if he had pulled this stuff before but didn't think so. She really would've heard if he had. Especially with Cinnamon always running her mouth.

The thought of Cinnamon made her uncomfortable, almost… guilty. Remorse was not her thing, and she wasn't even sure she recognized it for what it was. She knew now that she hadn't only been killing bad people, she was just killing. Like a cat torturing a bird with no intention of eating it, just play, for the pure fun of it. She had been killing out of anger on her own behalf, and it hadn't really bothered her. She wasn't sure she had ever killed someone for what they had done to other people. Steve had never really tried to pull anything like this on her. He was just leery enough of her to know better. For some reason, she could not let this stand. Steve was going to die, and it was going to hurt. A lot. If she did it right, she could probably make it look like the boss did it. After all, they'd already cut off a finger. She would just finish what they started. Pick up where they left off. Although she didn't think she was going to start with a finger.

Chapter Thirty-Seven

Frank knew someone was following him, but he didn't know if he should be worried about the guy on foot or the pair in the car as he hurried to his apartment.

By the time he was inside, the door locked and his weapon checked and loaded, the knock came.

Frank was going to ignore it, stay quiet and hope they left.

He figured the two in the car were Santonelli goons. He had no clue who'd been following on the street at a discreet distance. It could be the killer. It could be the landlord wanting his money. It could be a number of others he'd pissed off over the years. It could be…

"Open up, Michi. It's J.C. and I'm in trouble."

Yes, you are, buddy, Frank thought. He opened the door a crack and made sure J.C. saw the gun. "Tyler's been looking for you. They found your car. Went through your apartment. Saw all the camera footage of you in the strip club… with the women before they died. The one you've been stalking. It doesn't look good, kid."

J.C. didn't look good, either. He was disheveled. His hair a mess, his eyes sunken like he hadn't slept in a month. His suit hung on his body. He'd definitely lost weight.

"Do you think I did it? Huh? Any of it?" J.C. looked back over his shoulder. "Let me in, shoot me in the head, or close the fucking door."

Frank thought about closing the door and calling Tyler, but then J.C. would be in the wind again. He was about to ask where he'd been but opened the door and motioned him inside. There'd be time for questions in a minute. First things first: was anyone in the hallway, coming up the stairs or the elevator? It was quiet for the moment.

J.C. fell onto the couch and closed his eyes as Frank closed and locked the door.

"I didn't do it," J.C. whispered. "I'm guilty of getting a little too close to a stripper. That's it."

Frank sat down and sighed. "They found blood on your vehicle. They'll tie you to at least one death."

"Bullshit." J.C. opened his eyes and stood. He began pacing on the worn carpet. "Someone set me up. I've been trying to find out who. I went off the grid. Followed Gus Santonelli. It's not a coincidence he's in town. His men, too. You know what I found?"

Frank stayed quiet. He still had the weapon in his hand. J.C. might not be the killer, but he was acting crazy at the moment. "It isn't safe being here. Santonelli's men are on the street. They likely saw you. They'll be coming upstairs. I wish you'd have taken the hand when Tyler offered it. We could've hid you in a motel on the outskirts of town."

"And then what? This planted evidence comes back, and Tyler slaps the cuffs on his own partner?" J.C. stared at Frank. "Yet another partner."

Frank shrugged. "He never arrested me. It wasn't that dramatic. I quit before they hung me out to dry, and tried to take Tyler down with me." He stood. They needed to leave.

Five minutes ago. "If we can make it down the hall, we can hide in an empty apartment. I have the key to it, too. Don't ask me how. Let's go."

J.C. wasn't listening. "I found a body in the desert."

"Which one? There are a hundred or so out there." Frank motioned for J.C. to follow. He stepped to the door and put an ear to it.

"The bouncer's body was buried. Two holes in his head. He watched me waiting for Venus in the parking lot," J.C. said.

Frank came back into the living room, knowing they were wasting precious time. "We can straighten all of this out once we're safe."

J.C. pulled his weapon from his shoulder holster and Frank jumped back, ready to shoot J.C. if he did something stupid.

"They're coming for me," J.C. said. "I don't want to kill both of them, though. Wound the first one through the door. I need him to talk. To tell me what he knows. Got it?"

Frank sighed. "Or we can go down the hall and ambush them when they bust in, and ruin my door. Which I'll have to pay for."

"I had to leave my car at the airport. Make it look like I was leaving town." J.C. shook his head. "That never works. I need sleep. We'll kill these two and then I need to rest."

"I thought we were wounding one?" Frank didn't like any of this plan. He wasn't going to shoot someone if he could help it. He wasn't a cop anymore. With his shady past, he'd go to prison for murdering two hitmen from The Family. He'd be dead meat behind bars, too. How long would it take before the long arm of the mobsters squeezed the life from his neck, while the guards turned away, counting their payoff? No thanks.

J.C. rubbed his eyes with his free hand. "I'm so tired."

Frank could hear the goons outside the door. He put a finger to his lips, as if they'd think Frank wasn't home.

"I just need more time to figure out who's killing the dancers," J.C. said.

Frank hissed for him to shut up. He went into the kitchen, trying to find the perfect spot to hide behind and not get shot as soon as the goons kicked down the door.

"Whose blood was it they found?" J.C. asked.

Frank couldn't remember offhand. He'd talked to Tyler a couple of hours ago but there had been so much information. Tyler had been forced to spill what he had so far to his boss, which wasn't much. Of course, the cat was out of the bag about J.C. being the main suspect. Tyler's loyalty put into question, yet again, about protecting his partner. At the least, a reprimand was in order. A suspension without pay. A public flogging if that wasn't enough.

"Listen… they're outside. Coming inside. Focus, dammit, or we're both dead." Frank put his hip against the wall next to his overflowing garbage can. It stunk. He swore, if he survived this mess, he'd tie it up and haul it down to the dumpster.

"I'm sorry I dragged you into this," J.C. said. He stood in the center of the room, spread his legs and got into his shooting stance. "And I'm sorry about your door, too."

Frank took a deep breath and held it.

"Hey, Michi, we know you're in there and we know you ain't alone," a goon said from the hallway. He hadn't even knocked yet. "Open up or we're coming in. We just wanna talk to you's guys."

It was one thing to die in a hail of bullets when he was on the job, doing something good for a while, or even dying because a jealous husband had figured out Frank was giving it better than that guy ever could, or killed because of a hundred other different more logical reasons.

Dying because a cop he barely knew, had only known for a few days, had screwed up. The guy hadn't actually killed anyone, as far as Frank could tell, but it didn't matter.

None of this mattered right now.

"Frank… we'll kick it in if you want, but we'd rather talk," the goon said. "Our boss will be so disappointed in you, Michi. He thought you were on the up and up. Know what I'm sayin', huh?"

Frank stood up. His legs were already cramping. "Maybe if I open the door they won't kill us. Worth a shot?"

J.C. pulled the trigger at the same moment the goons started to kick in the door.

Chapter Thirty-Eight

J.C. had been in a fog. He'd been watching on the sidelines as his world spun out of control, all because he couldn't keep it in his pants. He'd been obsessed with a stripper, and now he was going to die. Why? Because he was an idiot.

The goons came in through the busted door, firing wildly.

J.C. dropped to his knees and fired until he was empty.

All hope of saving one of them to question went out the window once the shooting began.

In the movies, a gun battle lasts ten minutes. In real life, in such close quarters, it took ten seconds.

Smoke filled the apartment. Something heavy and glass fell in the kitchen behind him and shattered.

The two goons had face-planted on the carpet, pools of blood seeping into the floor and spreading out.

J.C. knew he'd been hit, a grazing shot on his left arm. He was bleeding but he didn't think it was life-threatening. Just enough to bother him. Annoy him.

Luckily, the goons had been unable to fully kick in the door as they rushed in. It allowed J.C. to get in a few shots that had hit the mark.

He kept his weapon drawn, even though it was empty, and pushed both men over with a foot. They were dead. Unseeing eyes staring at the dirty ceiling.

They carried no identification. Not even cash. He wondered if they'd left their wallets in the car downstairs, but neither had the keys on them.

Newer cars had those keypad locks. Maybe they had the keys in the car, but you needed to know the code to get in. It would be very convenient in the event one of them was killed and the other needed to make a quick getaway. Of course, with both dead, the likely rental would sit on the street until the city eventually towed it or the rental agency came looking for it.

Did they have trackers in the new cars, too? So the rental agency could easily locate it, in a casino parking lot or at a strip club or brothel, and repossess it if need be?

The groan brought J.C. back to the present. His mind was wandering again. The adrenaline was wearing off, and he was tired and hungry.

J.C. was breathing heavily, and he tried to control it but failed.

When he saw the blood covering Frank's torso, and his fading look, J.C. moaned.

"I'll call for an ambulance," J.C. said. "It's not that bad," he lied.

Frank frowned. "Bullshit," he whispered.

J.C. took Frank's phone from his pocket and called 9-1-1. When dispatch started asking questions, he hung up the phone. He knew as soon as Tyler heard Frank Michi had been shot, he'd be on his way.

J.C. went back to Frank. It seemed like the right thing to do. The man was dying, and it was his fault. The goons had followed J.C. in and a stray bullet had hit Frank.

At least it isn't from my gun, J.C. thought. *But it might as well have been, because I'm the reason he's dead.* "I am so sorry, Frank. Words cannot... I didn't kill those women."

Frank nodded his head slightly. He was in pain but still alive, still fighting to stay alive.

"Tyler will be coming. You tell him I didn't kill them. Can you do that?"

"He knows," Frank said before coughing. "Go find out who did this," he finally added.

"I think I know." J.C. stood.

Frank closed his eyes. "I'm so cold."

In the distance, J.C. could hear the sirens. He ran out, looking up and down the street for their car. Every car parked on the street looked the same. None of them had a giant sign pointing at it. He'd need to stay on foot and hope for the best.

Why did you abandon your damn car so soon? I should have hidden it in a nearby garage, J.C. thought. He knew it made no sense. How was he to know he'd eventually wind up at Frank's place, and have to shoot his way out? If he'd been thinking straight, J.C. knew the best move had been to drive as far away as possible. Get some sleep and food. Find a motel that took cash and think.

No time to think now, though. The police sirens were getting closer. He'd need to duck down an alley and hope the cops, the men and women he worked with up until this moment, weren't going to immediately canvas the area.

J.C. kept his head down. He didn't run, tried not to look like he was keeping an eye out for anyone noticing him. It was dark. In a shady area of town. People kept their mouths shut and didn't see anything, even if it happened right in front of them.

With any luck, he could walk for miles without anyone noticing him. He'd need to stay away from as many cameras as possible, which was nearly impossible in Las Vegas. Every store had one, and so did every casino. He knew the main thoroughfares did as well.

He'd be seen sooner than later on a surveillance system, and then the hunt would really be on. J.C. tried to figure out his options: try for a bus out of town, Uber as far as he could go, try to find a safe place to hide for a few days, or turn himself in.

"I'm innocent," J.C. whispered. "I didn't kill anyone."

You killed two men busting down a door. Frank Michi's death is on your hands, too. His blood is on your clothes, too, you idiot. This is not going to end well, J.C. thought.

He toyed with the idea of calling Tyler and trying to explain what had happened, but his mind was so jumbled right now. What had happened?

Shit. What if I did kill them? What if I was leading a double life, my body not under my control all the time, J.C. thought. *There's a demon inside calling the shots. I don't remember the deaths, but that doesn't mean I didn't do it. Right? Maybe I'm the killer.*

He knew it wasn't possible, but he found it harder and harder to focus. He was tired. Hungry. Food and sleep kept running through his head.

The neon signs were everywhere, the brightest city in the world. You could see it from space. Bothering his heavy eyes. Showing off the drops of blood on his clothes.

A long block away, after stumbling a couple of times, but not hearing sirens closing in on him, J.C. entered an all-night diner. It was a hole in the wall place, with greasy tables and greasy menus.

"Coffee and a water, please and thank you," J.C. mumbled to the waitress as she approached. He wanted to keep everyone as far away as possible. He looked down at his hands and saw the blood.

Irritated and embarrassed, J.C. rushed to the bathroom. He washed his face, tried his best to get the obvious bloodstains from his clothes. He couldn't look at himself in the mirror.

What have you done? Your life is over.

He exited the bathroom, expecting a police-issue weapon in his face.

Instead, he was alone. The other customers had left, and he saw the waitress and cook near the open back door as he peered into the kitchen.

As soon as J.C. looked at them, they fled.

"I'll get my own coffee, thanks," J.C. said. "You're not getting a tip, though."

He went behind the counter and poured himself some coffee. The first sip was like heaven. It warmed him up, gave him renewed life. Even if it was going to be fleeting before his body succumbed to everything happening.

Everything I did to get to this point.

There was food being cooked. Scrambled eggs. Hash browns. Toast popped in the toaster.

"Don't mind if I do," J.C. said. He started to plate the food, smiling when he was finished and slapped the bell with his hand. "Order up."

J.C. sat down with his food and coffee and dug in. This might be his last real meal for a long time.

He heard the sirens in the distance.

Chapter Thirty-Nine

Just before last call, Venus found Lexi in the dressing room. She was getting dressed and packing up her stuff. Steve was lurking just outside the door.

"I think he's waiting for me," Lexi whimpered.

"That's ok, he probably is, but we're going to walk out together. If he tries to tell you to go to the office, I'll intervene. You'll be ok. Just keep your head down and let me handle it. He won't want to piss me off. He needs me too much," Venus said, her rage was becoming harder and harder to control.

She knew she was right. They were too short on girls to want to lose one that always came in when asked, didn't get fucked up at work, and maintained regular customers. It's definitely why Steve hadn't tried this shit on her. He made a few subtle advances at first, but she was used to it, and was able to hold him off until he found a new target. It was guys like this that made this job hard. She would handle him, though, piece by piece.

"If you avoid him long enough, he'll lose interest and move on," Venus assured her.

Lexi was damn cute. She didn't think Steve would actually give up that easily, but that was ok. She really only needed to get Lexi out the door this one night.

The new girl looked relieved, and Venus was glad to help. It seemed she might have a conscience after all. If only an itty bitty one. The last few weeks and days had really given her time to think. Although she didn't really feel all that bad about the people she had killed, many of them were on sketchy paths anyway. She didn't like that she had killed more for her own ego. She was irritated with herself for justifying her own vanity, and even more irritated that she could be such a fool as to delude herself. Helping out Lexi did feel like the right thing. Instead of painting herself the hero, the selfless public servant, she thought she may just take on the role of karmic assistant. Just help things along a bit, while feeding her own lust for blood.

"Ok," Lexi said, as she packed up her things. Venus was ready to go as well, another advantage to not wearing elaborate costumes. Venus opened the door and was relieved to see that Steve was over by the bar and not stalking the dressing room. He was watching as they moved toward the exit though.

"Hey Lexi," Steve said, obviously trying to sound not douchey and obviously failing. "How'd it go tonight? Why don't you come talk to me in the office?"

"We're going to go have breakfast, Steve. Lexi's got a few things to learn about Vegas," Venus said, as she took Lexi's hand and could feel the girl trembling. She quickened her pace toward the front door, where a large bouncer named Andy was waiting to grab their bags.

"Well, ok. Lexi, I'll catch you tomorrow night," Steve said and gave a grotesque wink that only served to fuel Venus' already burning fury.

Andy took their bags and opened the front door, allowing the two women to exit first. Chivalry had not quite breathed its last breath.

He walked them to their respective cars, and before she said goodbye, Venus told Lexi to be careful and stick close to her for the next few shifts. Knowing that she was not exactly telling the truth. In the next hour or so, Steve would no longer be a problem. Lexi still looked concerned, and that was exactly how she wanted her to be. What a lovely coincidence it will be for her to show up tomorrow to Mike the DJ filling in as manager. He was too coked out most of the time to demand a blowjob.

Minnie pulled out of the parking lot, wearing a slight smile. She pulled into an alleyway close by where there would be no cameras. She knew that Steve would be the last to leave and lock up. The rest of the staff would likely be meeting for breakfast somewhere and would be in a hurry to get out of there.

As she waited, she checked to see what supplies she had in her car. Once again she found herself unprepared. If she drove home now, she could get caught on a camera or two, and would most likely miss Steve closing up the club. It made her uncomfortable, but there was an underlying thrill to it also. Her usual method consisted of meticulous planning and consideration, but the last few times had not been that. It was definitely a challenge, and she was enjoying it, but her anxiety was high.

She checked her trunk first. She had all the things a single woman should have. A tire iron, utility knife, a sweet little pair of pliers with a wire cutter, and a pair of gloves, of course. A lady wouldn't want to mess up her manicure changing a tire. She wasn't sure she could dismember a body quickly with what she had, but she could definitely make it hurt. She might have to get creative.

She put the knife in her waistband and the pliers and gloves in her pocket. Her excitement was building now, and much like her anger, it would be difficult to control. Minnie started for the club, keeping in the shadows. She came around the back of the club and found the power box, hoping she wasn't on camera. If she was being recorded it wouldn't be for very long. She wasn't sure which wires to cut so she cut them all.

Feeling a little more in control, she found her way to the side door, which opened to the hallway where the office was located. She rolled her eyes as she found it unlocked and stepped right in.

The hallway was dark, lit only by the emergency lights. She heard a loud bang and then Steve say "Fuck!"

Minnie moved toward the office door, which was still closed. She was just about to pull out her knife, when she noticed the fire extinguisher in a case next to the door. A shiny new axe rested next to it. She grabbed the little hammer on the chain next to the case and in two quick moves, smashed the glass and freed the axe. She didn't wait for Steve to make any noise, and turned the knob on the office door and burst in.

Steve had already come out from behind the desk, and even in the low light she could see look of surprise on his stupid face. When she saw the gun in his hand, it was her turn to be surprised. *This appears to be your lucky day, fuckhead,* she thought as she swung the axe, burying the business end in the side of his head just above his ear. He didn't have time to bring up the gun, as his body started to fall to the floor. He landed with a thud, and Minnie kicked the gun away from his hand. That appeared to be unnecessary, considering he had a good two inches of steel in his brain.

She stared down at the spreading pool of blood and found she was disappointed that she hadn't gotten to take her time. She had been so looking forward to picking up where the guys from back east and his goons had left off. Although, had she hesitated, she might have caught a bullet. That was a mean looking gun on the floor. She had never had much of a taste for guns. She had taken a class or two at a gun range when she got to Vegas just to have basic knowledge, but when it came to dispatching human beings, using a gun felt like cheating. She preferred to get her hands dirty.

She walked over to it now, and inspected it. It was locked and loaded. Her adrenaline was still coursing through her body. Minnie was not pleased at how close to death she had come in the last few days.

Minnie was thinking about her next move. Under normal circumstances, she would have already known. Now she was just staring at the now deceased douchey Steve, the lucky sonofabitch. She had been thinking about cutting off his dick and sticking it in his mouth. She thought that would make it look like the bosses had done it. *Did mobsters do that outside of the movies?* Either way, it would've been fun.

Lost in thought about dismembered members, she almost missed the sound of movement outside the door. It had swung shut while she was dealing with Steve. She was empty-handed with the axe still buried in Steve's skull, so she started to reach for the gun as the door knob turned.

Chapter Forty

Tyler had never been much of a daredevil driver before or after joining the police force. Now, he drove like his ass was on fire. His siren and lights weren't enough to get the traffic out of his way, and he drove onto the sidewalk a couple of times, scraped against a minivan in an intersection and scared quite a few tourists wandering around town looking to lose their money.

He rushed up the stairs to Frank's apartment and frowned when he saw two officers already inside, both staring at the scene before them.

"Don't touch anything," Tyler yelled, flashing his badge. "Did you call an ambulance?"

"On the way."

Tyler surveyed the scene. Two men down. Shot. He saw Frank on the ground and took a deep breath. "No one in or out until I say so. My scene."

Both cops nodded and stepped into the hallway, likely glad to be out of the apartment. It stunk like blood, shit and the lingering smoke of a firefight.

Tyler put on a pair of gloves and knelt next to Frank, who opened his eyes wide.

For a second Tyler thought his old partner was going to make it, might still be able to pull through, but then he saw how much blood he'd lost. His skin was pale and he was sweaty. His eyes focused and unfocused and he moved his lips to speak but nothing came out.

"Who did this, Frank?" Tyler leaned forward. He felt like he was in a bad movie, and his dying friend would tell him everything.

And he did.

"J.C.… he…" Frank spit up blood and closed his eyes, convulsing.

"Move," an EMT yelled at Tyler, who fell back on his ass on the carpet. He watched as the crew surrounded Frank.

Tyler walked as quickly as possible to the stairwell, where he puked. Two cops coming up stopped at the landing below. "That bad, Detective Fitt?"

Tyler could only nod, catching his breath by the time the two got to his level. "Frank Michi. My old partner."

"Jeez. Sorry, man. Know who did it?"

Tyler hesitated. He shook his head. The only thing that made sense was J.C. was there, with Frank, and they fought off the goons. He knew beyond a shadow of a doubt the two dead men worked for The Family and Gus Santonelli. If he was a betting man, he'd know what had happened: J.C. and Frank were in the apartment when the two goons kicked down the door and everyone started firing.

The question he had was a big one. Had J.C. and Frank been on the same side, or had The Family gotten a jump on J.C. before he had time to kill Frank? For that matter, what if J.C. had already shot Frank? But then the question remained… Why kill Frank?

Tyler shook his head. It made no sense. Ballistics would give it all a nice timeline and stamp, and then it would all make perfect sense. Except Tyler didn't know if they had time for all of that.

Where was J.C. right now?

He closed his eyes and tried to get his focus back. He was a cop, dammit. A very good detective. He'd solved worse cases. He'd been in it thicker than this, too. Especially the times Frank crossed the line and he had to cross it along with him to save his partner's ass.

His old partner who was dead, his new partner who might've killed him.

This was worse than The Incident.

He heard the voice of Sergeant Edler on the nearest officer's radio and he put out his hand. Tyler knew he'd ask if he was there, and wanted an immediate update. Tyler was wondering why he wasn't already here.

"I'm here," Tyler said, trying not to sound tired. Knowing he'd failed. "This is FUBAR, sarge."

"Tell me what happened."

Tyler knew that meant no guesses. Edler wanted the facts and only the facts. Guessing about a crime got you nowhere, and Tyler knew back in his day, Sergeant Edler had been a damn fine cop. Unfortunately, now he was mired in the politics of his position and aiming to keep going higher. He was already in the mayor's pocket, if the rumors were true.

"Two goons. Members of The Family. They kicked in the door and began shooting," Tyler said.

"Shooting at who?"

Tyler took a deep breath. Tried to relax. Separate himself from this mess. Be a professional. "Frank Michi and J.C. Forrestt."

"Survivors?"

"J.C., but he isn't here," Tyler said. "The other three are dead."

There it was. Frank Michi, who he'd known for so many years, was dead. Why? Because Tyler had dragged him into this, kicking and screaming, bribing him with C.I.

money because he knew Frank needed it. He'd used his old partner. Old friend. For what? In the end he'd been blinded by the facts, which were staring him in the face. His gut had done him wrong.

J.C. might be the killer. Again… where was he?

"I'm sorry for your loss, Fitt. I know you and Michi had a bond, which is rare, especially once one of the pair walks off," Edler said. "Any idea where J.C. went off to? We have his car. It's processed and the blood matches one of the victims. It isn't looking good."

Tyler was at a loss. Where had J.C. gone? If he were smart, he'd leave town. If he was really smart, he would've left already, though.

He glanced back inside the apartment just as they put a sheet over Frank's body.

"I'll find him," Tyler said through gritted teeth. He had no idea where to begin. He'd need to get officers to the bus station, the airport, every major road out. He'd need a hundred men. It seems impossible.

Sergeant Edler didn't respond and Tyler thought he'd lost the radio signal.

"Are you still there?" Tyler was already moving. He needed to get away and start looking. He'd form a taskforce. There was no use denying it: J.C. was their man. He'd be dragged onto the carpet when this was all over, and the politicians would wonder why he hadn't seen it coming. Question his loyalty to the department. Wonder if he was a part of this. The Incident would be dredged up again, and with Frank dead, directly because of his involvement, he'd lose his badge. His life.

"Detective Fitt, I think we caught a break," Edler said.

Tyler realized he'd walked off with the officer's radio. He'd get it back later.

"We have eyes on J.C. if the caller can be believed," Sergeant Edler said. "Here's the address. He's in a diner not too far from where you're at."

Tyler felt like he'd been struck by lightning. He stopped short and caught his breath. "Nobody moves until I get there. Is that clear?"

Despite outranking Tyler, Sergeant Edler agreed. "Hurry. Who knows what he's going to do, Fitt."

Chapter Forty-One

Minnie found herself face down, ass up reaching for Steve's gun as the big boss from back east came into the room. She grabbed the gun and spun around to face him. He looked like a big burly grizzly bear, and she was staring right into the barrel of a firearm that made Steve's gun look like a kid's toy.

Santo-spaghetti? she thought lamely, as she hefted the gun to aim it at the large man. She had only heard his name whispered once or twice in passing. In her head, she swept her right leg up in a swift and graceful move to knock the gun out of his hand. In reality, she kicked her leg much too high, missing his hand altogether while losing her balance and falling squarely on her ass. Her own gun discharged, lodging a bullet in the ceiling as the kickback it sent flying out of her hand and across the room, landing well beyond her reach.

Santonelli smiled a terrible smile and holstered his own gun. He bent down over her and began to put his enormous hands around her neck.

"It would be a shame to blow apart such a pretty face," he said menacingly, as he began to strangle her.

She fought for breath as she wondered how in the fuck she ended up like this? Minnie had never found herself in this kind of predicament before, and was starting to think this might just be the end of her. *Fuck all that.* She silenced her nihilistic thoughts and kicked her foot up, hoping to reach his crotch. Succeeding in lightly tapping his balls with the tip of her toe. He shifted slightly, making his genitals a harder target.

Minnie's strength was waning now as her lungs started to burn. She struggled to keep her eyes open. She reached up with both hands and managed to poke one acrylic tipped finger into his eye. He squinted, and his hands stayed around her neck and loosened just a little, but enough for her to wriggle into a better position to land her sneaker clad foot directly into his balls.

The big bad man screamed like a little girl and let go of her neck. Cool air flooded her flaming lungs as she took a deep breath. She braced herself on her left foot and swung her right with as much force as she could and kicked him square in the face. Not in any way close to the graceful smooth move she had wanted to mimic from the action movies she had watched but effective just the same. His nose exploded in a gushing torrent of blood.

The large guy was bent over, holding his nose but starting to recover. Before the behemoth could get a hand on his really large gun, Minnie wrenched the axe from Steve's skull. She swung it without aiming and hit Santonelli directly in the gut, producing a squishy wet sound that sent her own stomach reeling.

The axe didn't stick into the fat and flesh like it had bone, but almost sucked into it instead. Had the axe not been as sharp, it might have just bounced back and hit her in the face. She pulled it back, flinging a large arch of blood across the room walls and ceiling. She swung it again, this time a little higher, hitting him in at the top of his arm close to his shoulder, almost severing it completely. He dropped to the floor in a wet heap.

Still fearing a bullet, she swung again, and again, and again. She had come here hoping for a good old fashioned slow dismemberment, but ending up chopping up a mob boss. *Maybe working on the fly isn't so bad?*

Covered in gore, she stared down at the pile of flesh that had apparently been quite the formidable crime boss. Her gaze turned to Steve whose eyes shared her own look of surprise. She thought she could see his brains trying to ooze onto the office floor, but she couldn't be sure. She wasn't sure what brains looked like outside of the horror movies. This whole incident had really highlighted her ignorance in certain areas. Wherever she ended up she intended on taking a more extensive firearms course, an anatomy class, and she definitely needed to learn some martial arts. She was grateful that the only person to witness that humiliating awkward kick was now resting in pieces on the floor. She might have hacked him up just for that even if he hadn't been trying to kill her.

Now, Minnie needed to figure out how to clean up two dead guys. She surveyed the room, which even in the almost darkness looked like quite the mess. There was no cleaning this up, not to mention, pinning Steve's death on the mobster was not going to happen now. *Looks like 'Lil Lexi is going to have to find another club in Vegas after all.* Minnie was going to burn this place to the ground.

First she was going to need to get out of these clothes. She wasn't just splattered with blood, she was soaked in it. She made her way out of the office and into the darkened club. The emergency lights were still on and provided her with just enough light to get to the dressing room. Back in the corner, she located the box which contained the lost and found items. It was mostly old stripper gear, but she managed to find a tiny t-shirt with Britney Spears' picture on the front of it, and a pair of way too big daisy dukes. Her shoes were kind of a problem as well. They were also covered, but unless she wanted to totter out of there on 8-inch light up plastic stilettos she would have to go barefoot. Better than leaving a trail of bloody footprints.

She stripped and washed off the blood in the sink, pulled the shorts and t-shirt on, cringing as her boobs distorted Britney's face. She preferred being covered in blood, but figured it was better than having to explain why she looked like she had just murdered someone with an axe. *Why yes officer, I did just murder someone with an axe.*

She stepped out of the dressing room for the last time and headed to the bar. She located a case of Everclear, which contained the highest alcohol content she could find, and began to pour it all around the floor. She tossed a bottle into the office and hallway, and when it ran out, she started on the vodka, and rubbing alcohol she found in the cleaning closet.

When she was done she decided it probably wouldn't hurt to bust all the hard liquor bottles open for good measure. Stopping to take a swig from a bottle of high-end bourbon that had a considerable layer of dust on it. Her next club would have to have a more discerning clientele. Minnie almost never drank, but then again she almost never murdered people without a plan.

Satisfied that the place would burn at least enough to cover her tracks, she grabbed a couple of Pink Pussycat complementary matchbooks from the bar. Starting in the dressing room and working her way toward the hallway door where she came in, she tossed lit matches in every nook and cranny of the club, ending with the horrific but oh so satisfying scene in the office. *Smell ya later assholes,* she thought with a grin as she threw several lit matches into the room. The rest of the club was already in flames as she stepped out of the door and into the night.

Chapter Forty-Two

Tyler walked into the diner, hands out and smiling.

J.C. was seated in a booth with a heaping plate of food and a cup of coffee next to his weapon. He nodded at Tyler.

Tyler took a few steps but J.C. put his hand up. "No closer. Take a seat at the table right there and put your hands on it. No sudden moves. If you go for your gun I'll have to kill you."

"No problem." Tyler sat down and did as he was instructed. The last thing he wanted to do was get into a gunfight. Especially in these close quarters.

The flashing red and blue lights in the parking lot were strobing onto the walls and ceiling. Tyler knew several snipers were set on rooftops and on the street, ready to shoot if J.C. made a sudden move.

"It's been a crazy few days, huh?" Tyler asked.

J.C. chuckled. "I guess we'll go through the motions of you setting a rapport with me. Gaining my trust. Make me rethink what's happening. I'm sure you're wired, too. Who's in charge? Is it Edler?"

Tyler nodded. "I'm not here to fake you out, lull you so you surrender. I want you to come to that conclusion, J.C. Are there hostages?"

J.C. looked at Tyler and frowned.

"There are. Two of them?" Tyler nodded subtly. If they knew J.C. was alone in the diner, they would open fire if he didn't give up. He had no leverage beside the weapon on the table next to his coffee cup. "Let's talk. Figure this out together."

Tyler was hoping to skirt around all of the gray area things he'd done during the investigation. He felt like shit for wanting to save his own career, but knew J.C. was a goner no matter what. Even if he wasn't the killer.

"Why'd you kill Frank?" Tyler asked, figuring he was wasting time. He wanted to get to the point, let J.C. know it was futile to keep this charade going, and surrender.

"I didn't. I went to Frank to talk. I needed an ally."

"You couldn't trust me?" Tyler asked.

J.C. shrugged. "There was so much going on. I did some really bad things." He lifted his coffee cup and put it back down. "Feel free to get a cup. We might be here awhile. Do it slowly and with your hands up."

"Hard to pour coffee from that angle," Tyler said and smiled, trying to lighten the mood. It didn't seem to work. "I'll skip coffee for now. Tell me about the two dead men in Frank's apartment."

"Goons from The Family. Santonelli in town. I'm sure he sent them." J.C. shook his head. "I followed her. I screwed up."

"Followed who?"

J.C. sighed and put his hand on the gun. "The dancer. I was obsessed with her. I followed her home. I went to a resort, too. Stalked her. I couldn't stop thinking about her."

"Venus," Tyler said.

J.C. nodded. "There's something about her."

"Did you do this to impress her? Have her scared so you'd be her knight in shining armor?"

J.C. sighed again. "It's complicated."

"Nothing is that complicated except women." Tyler wanted a cup of coffee now but didn't dare make a sudden move. He glanced out the window and saw the multitude of fellow officers, all ready to pounce.

"I need you to bring him out, Fitt," Sergeant Edler said in his earpiece. "We're running out of time. Where are the hostages? We don't have a visual on them. If they're in the back, we can take him out now. You know the signal."

Tyler was supposed to put his hands on his face if he thought he'd lost control and there was no other choice than a sniper taking out J.C.

It will never come to that, Tyler thought. *I'm not going to watch them kill him in front of me. Even if he draws down on me.*

J.C. smiled and tapped the side of his head. "They getting antsy already?"

Tyler nodded. "It would be nice and easy if you let me extract you. I'll take you personally downtown and we can chat. It doesn't have to go any farther than this."

J.C. still had one hand on the weapon but picked up his fork and took a bite of his food. "Last supper," he muttered.

"It doesn't have to be," Tyler said. "Whatever you've done, we can sort it out. You know that. A good lawyer in Vegas is a dime a dozen. You'll get through this."

"No matter what I've done?" J.C. glanced at Tyler and took another bite. "Do you think I killed those strippers?"

"I'm not sure right now," Tyler admitted. "We can figure it out."

"They found blood on my car. My apartment might be filled with clues. Bodies piling up and I'm not accounted for. I get it." J.C. put the fork down. "I'm guilty and it doesn't matter if I did it or not."

"It does matter."

J.C. looked tired. He slumped in the booth but picked up the gun and stared at it. "She played me. Had me thinking I was going to have something special with her. Led me on. I wonder if she thought I was the killer. Maybe being nice to me so she could live. Thinking it was better to sleep with a serial killer than be the next victim."

"Holy shit, did he just admit it?" Edler in Tyler's ear.

Tyler put his hands up. "Did you do this, J.C.? Did you kill those women?"

J.C. shook his head. "Whoever did is still out there, partner. Frank knew it. Maybe he knew who it was, too. Is he still alive?"

When Tyler didn't answer, J.C. groaned.

"We're going to come in," Sergeant Edler said. "Get the weapon secured. You have a minute."

"No," Tyler said under his breath.

J.C. smiled faintly. "They're coming in. They want you to secure the gun." He held it up near his face. "This isn't going to end well for any of us."

Tyler got ready to spring. If J.C. turned the gun on him, he'd need to lunge and attempt to tackle him. He wasn't about to play into his hands of death by cop, the coward's way out.

"I never told you how much I enjoyed our short time together. I learned a lot from you, Tyler. You're a damn good cop. Too good, in fact. You care too much and aren't afraid to cut through the politics and bullshit to do your job. I wish this had been different," J.C. and put the gun barrel in his mouth.

Tyler was up and took a step before the weapon was discharged.

Chapter Forty-Three

Three dancers in a row had strutted out to a Bon Jovi song. Tyler didn't care, though. It all blended in together tonight. He'd drink himself to oblivion and hope he could find his way back home.

He'd been put on leave with pay, but had a sinking feeling it would end up being a permanent vacation from his job. He'd weathered some gray area things in his career, definite illegal moves as well, but he'd always skated by. Just out of reach, while others took a fall.

Not this time. Tyler waved at the bartender for another drink.

A dancer sidled up to him at the bar with a perfect smile to match her perfect tits and ass.

"Hey, wanna dance?"

Tyler shrugged. He wasn't in the mood. He didn't want company and didn't want to get all worked up over nothing, leaving the strip club with less money and a raging hard-on.

She stared at him, her smile never faltering. Finally, she looked past him and wandered to the next guy at the bar.

The Bon Jovi song ended and Whitesnake began, the dancer in a frenzy now as she moved suggestively around the pole.

He'd stayed away from the clubs on the other side of town, especially the Pink Pussycat. It would look even worse for him if he was caught on camera in that shithole.

How far the mighty have fallen, Tyler thought. He'd barely slept. Hadn't eaten in a couple of days, and the beer was going right to his head. He was going to slowly kill every last brain cell and he didn't give a shit.

He'd seen the look on Sergeant Edler as he'd been called into the office, everyone in the bullpen trying not to stare and failing.

"I need your gun and badge," the sergeant had said simply. As if anything else needed to be said. Tyler had declined having a rep with him, knowing it would only prolong the inevitable.

At the door, Sergeant Edler had cleared his throat. "Why don't you get out of town for a few days? You're getting paid. I made sure of it. Go to Los Angeles. Go see the Grand Canyon, Fitt. This isn't your fault, but there's a process, as you know."

Tyler had thanked him and left, ignoring the looks as he did the walk of shame to his car.

Instead of getting out of town and running from his problems, he'd spent a lot of time on the couch. Ordering takeout food. Drinking every last ounce of beer and the harder stuff until he was out. Finally venturing back into society, even if it was on the outskirts.

The song stopped and before the next one, Tyler thought it might've been a Def Leppard song, he heard the dancer who'd tried to get him into the VIP room and hand over his money, say something interesting.

"Yeah, I worked at the club where all the dancers were killed by that cop. I'm here because it burned to the ground," she said.

Tyler slipped off of his chair, nearly falling to the floor. He tapped her on the shoulder.

The guy she was talking to didn't look too happy, and stood up.

If Tyler had had his weapon on him, he would've clubbed the guy. Instead, he used his beer and clocked the asshole in the face.

The dancer looked shocked but no one else in the strip club had seen it or didn't really care.

"Tell me what you told him," Tyler said.

"I… don't know what you're talking about… don't hurt me." She was looking around, trying to get the attention of the bouncers.

Tyler took out his wallet and waved two twenties. "Can I get that dance now?"

She smiled, as if nothing had happened, and led him back through the curtains.

Despite him wanting information from her, he was tired and hungry. And horny. He watched as she straddled him, an inch from their crotches touching. She grinned and licked her lips as she swayed in time to the music.

Tyler closed his eyes and felt himself drifting off into oblivion. It would be so easy to give in and stop caring. What did it matter if it was the Pink Pussycat that had burned to the ground? Another move by J.C. to cover his tracks. Only…

He opened his eyes. She hadn't even noticed he'd nearly fallen out, her back to him gyrating her tight ass. She was moving to the rhythm, and he was caught in its trance.

"Hey, hold on a second," Tyler said, clearing his throat. He looked up at the ceiling and wished his bulge wasn't so obvious. "Did you say you'd worked at the Pink Pussycat?"

She stopped moving and stared at Tyler. He knew she was wondering whether to answer her or run.

Tyler knew if he said he was a cop, or had been a cop at this point, she'd bolt. He smiled and put up his hands. "I'm just a guy who enjoys going to the clubs to have a drink and get a dance. Curious. I hadn't heard it was on fire."

She eyed the money in his hand and he slipped her a twenty, which she tucked away in the front of her thong deftly. "Yeah, a few days ago. Torched. They said it was arson. Found the bodies inside."

"The bodies?"

She nodded. "Steve, the owner, and some other guy. Someone had broken the bottles and set it all on fire. Probably the cop who killed those girls. Right?"

"Probably," Tyler said. He extended his hand. "Thanks for the information. I appreciate it."

She shook his hand. "You're welcome. I'm Lexi. Don't you want me to finish?"

Tyler grinned. "I think I'm done. You're very good. I'll see you again." He gave her the other twenty and waited until she left to adjust himself and leave the club.

He was suddenly sober. He stood on the sidewalk and looked it up on his phone, reading a couple of different articles about the mysterious arson.

The timeline doesn't work out, Tyler thought. *It happened while J.C. was already at the diner. The fire has to be connected to the murders. Cleaning it up, wiping the last traces away.*

He ran back inside and found Lexi right before she was heading to the back with another guy.

"Hey, uh, quick question… whatever happened to the other dancers? Did they all move over to this place?" Tyler asked.

She cocked her head and frowned. "Almost all of us."

"Who didn't?"

"Venus," Lexi said. "She was really nice to me. Helped me out of a jam with Steve, the owner, the guy who was killed in the fire."

Tyler couldn't breathe. He stumbled back outside and went in search of Venus, who he thought was the key to all of this.

The one who knew a lot more than she'd been telling.

Chapter Forty-Four

"Give it up, give it up, give it up for the beautiful Karma!" the DJ said into the mic, feigning excitement. *Yeah, boys give it up,* she thought, as she collected her tips amid a flurry of applause and whistles. She swept the bills into a pile and scooped the whole thing up in both hands before making her way through the curtain and down the stairs off stage. Her first Saturday night at a high end strip club in Atlantic City was proving to be a good one. She was sure that the top shelf liquor in this place didn't sit around collecting dust.

She gave a quick head nod to the girl climbing the steps to the stage as she struggled to contain the large handfuls of bills that seemed determined to slip out of her hands. She reached her spot in the dressing room and let them spill out on the counter, catching a glimpse of herself in the mirror as she did.

After two weeks, her new image still startled her. Her formerly flaming hair was now a deep golden blonde. She had never thought of herself as a blonde, but it went well with her skin tone and she was starting to like it. New look, new life. Sort of.

Atlantic City held many of the same charms and vices as Vegas, but it could not boast to have a smoldering pile of ashes that had once been a strip club. At least not yet. She liked it here so far. As in Vegas, she rented a fully furnished apartment. Not having to lug a sofa and bed across the country made moving a breeze. She simply stuffed all her belongings in her car, Jeff included, told the management she wouldn't be back, and bailed.

She would've loved to be able to have recreated her *regular* self as she did her *stripper* persona, but the process of obtaining the proper licenses had left her social security number and fingerprints on file. It also meant she couldn't just skip town without tying up her loose ends, and needed to keep a squeaky clean record. Despite being in a profession that left her often in the company of misfits and questionable characters, Minerva had never had so much as a parking ticket. Her credit score was spectacular and her tax returns were immaculate. On paper she was Mary fucking Poppins. If Mary Poppins happened to be a stripper, that is.

It didn't take her long to settle into a new place and Atlantic City was just as good a place to be anonymous as Las Vegas. Almost better in some respects. She was more accustomed to the western part of the country and the food here took some getting used to. She still wasn't certain what the hell a pork roll was and also wasn't certain she really wanted to know. Jeff of course hated everything, but seemed to resolve to acclimate just the same.

The cremation of the Pink Pussycat had been but a blip on the news. In Las Vegas, where the implosion of buildings was a spectator sport, the only real exciting thing had been the bodies found. And even that wasn't that exciting. A sleazy strip club manager and a well known if not always acknowledged mob figure roasted in an alcohol fueled fire was rather droll, and not great for tourism. The stripper killings stopped, some bad dudes were dead. Let the liquor flow and suckers place their bets.

Her blonde hair had been cut to just below her shoulders and complimented her pale skin nicely. She caught herself staring right about the time it might appear creepy to anyone paying attention. She focused her attention to straightening out the pile of bills in front of her, flattening each one out and facing them in a pile. She took a moment to mourn Jake, who would've done this for her. It wouldn't take long for her to find another Jake, though. She was already developing the same reputation for no bullshit as she always had. A few more generous tips and they would be lining up to lick her feet again.

Her metamorphosis went well beyond her physical appearance. She built a new facade, a mask for who she was, a clever deception she presented to the world. She was a killer. A very good one, in fact. She came to realize that the killings that were done in the name of her own vanity had gotten her close to getting caught and even killed herself. What happened in Vegas would die in Vegas, but the lesson would live on.

Sass's murder had unnerved and rattled her because it meant that she was weak, selfish and full of jealous rage. Not a good look. Burying the axe in Steve's head, well that had been exhilarating. She stared Death in the face and told him to eat shit. That was the badass she wanted to be, not beating a poor stripper to death over some strip club customer and a bruised ego. Besides, she had broken a nail in the process.

She wouldn't break any more nails killing helpless strippers and bartenders who talked too much. She would only use her skills on the most deserving of prey. The ones who made it exciting, the ones whose blood fueled her passion. She didn't think she would have to do much hunting, either. Given her job, they would come to her.

Her bills were now neatly stacked, but not counted, and she picked them up to be deposited in her locker. She applied fresh lip gloss, body spray, and took a long swig of water before closing the door. The dressing room was buzzing with the noise of young girls hoping to make their fortunes or possibly simply marry into one. And yes, even a few making their tuition for the quarter in the hope they might be able to quit with a few extra letters after their names. *Grind on my friends,* she thought as she left the dressing room.

The club itself was indistinguishable from most clubs. Fake smoke from the fog machine helped to hide the obnoxious pattern on the carpet. She suspected but had never confirmed that all the clubs bought their upholstery and carpet from the same outlet. Some maybe slightly less nauseating than the others, but all intended to conceal vomit and cigarette burns.

She stood next to the DJ booth and surveyed the room, overwhelmed by her choice of intoxicated targets. She was starting to prioritize, as she became aware of conversation behind her. Curious, she listened.

"Please, I can't go up again. Dave said I could leave. I've been here since noon and haven't made shit. I want to go home," a very young stripper said to the DJ.

"I don't give a fuck what Dave said, and I don't give a fuck that you already tipped the day DJ. You were here for part of my shift and you owe me. Get your ass on stage, and make me my tip, or you can forget working my shifts again," Paul the DJ said.

She hadn't seen the girl before, but then again, she hadn't seen most of the girls before. She had jet black hair and a slim build. She had to have been at least 21 but didn't look a day over 16. She had met Paul at the beginning of the shift, and he had refused to even look her in the eye when she checked in. But was soon her best friend in the world when she had gotten his attention long enough to hand him a couple of twenties.

"Please, I barely made my car payment, I just can't give out anymore," the girl had started to cry. "I'll get you double next time," she continued.

"The fuck you will. Go ahead, get the fuck out of here, but you won't work any of my shifts again," Paul said.

She turned to appear to look at another part of the room in time to see Paul dismiss the girl with a wave of his hand. She backed down the stairs and started heading toward the dressing room. DJ's were the deities of the strip club. They held a disproportionate amount of power. They controlled the lighting, the music, and a DJ could make or break a dancer. A good portion of the time they were assholes, something most girls learned the first few nights. Some thrived on the position and used it as leverage for sexual favors as well as tips. Most DJ's made more money than the dancers. Some DJ's were disgusting greedy pigs.

Karma wore a slight smile as she walked away from the DJ booth and toward an inebriated bachelor party in the middle of the room. She thought she was really going to like it here.

ABOUT THE AUTHORS

Armand Rosamilia is a New Jersey boy currently living in sunny Florida, where he writes when he's not sleeping. He's happily married to a woman who helps his career and is supportive, which is all he ever wanted in life...

He's written over 150 stories that are currently available, including horror, zombies, contemporary fiction, thrillers and more. His goal is to write a good story and not worry about genre labels.

He not only runs two successful podcasts...

Arm Cast Podcast - interviewing fellow authors as well as filmmakers, musicians, etc.

The Mando Method Podcast with co-host Chuck Buda - talking about writing and publishing

But he owns the network they're on, too! Project Entertainment Network

He also loves to talk in third person... because he's really that cool.

You can find him at https://armandrosamilia.com for not only his latest releases but interviews and guest posts with other authors he likes!

Erin Louis is a former adult entertainer with three non-fiction books about her life as a stripper as well as several short fiction stories.

She has a lifelong love of horror and dark humor.

Please check out her website at https://www.erinlouis.com/

Other HellBound Books Titles
Available at:
www.hellboundbookspublishing.com

South of the Mason-Dixon

When Harrison returned to his small hometown for the first time in years, he thought he knew what to expect but couldn't have been more wrong.

When Andy immigrated from South Korea to the U.S., he never would have guessed his first taste of America could be so foul.

Together, these newlyweds are thrust into a fight for survival and will find out just how deep the roots of homophobia go.

Brat out of Hell

John Milton, some famous dead guy, once wrote that it was better to rule in Hell than to serve in Heaven. What if you weren't too keen on either? That's the position in which Danasdius, demon prince, grandson of Lucifer finds himself.

In fact, what he'd really like is to have a nice, normal life on Earth.

So, he does the only thing he can think of: he runs away from Hell.

Decades later, his unobservant, often absentee father, Moraspus, has noticed the palace is a bit quieter than usual and decides to get Danasdius back.

Can Dan and the friends he's made on earth make sure he stays a BRAT OUT OF HELL?

The Amityville Murder House

Jen Dodd is annoyed when her husband, Josh, drags her from Wichita, Kansas, to Amityville, New York, to tour two supposedly-haunted houses. But she's far more annoyed when he purchases one of the houses, forcing her to move across the country.

The Dodd family's new home, dubbed by locals as "The Murder House," is located across town from the *Amityville Horror* house that became famous in the 1970s. Despite having never heard of "The Murder House" before starting this journey, Jen will soon learn that it's far more dangerous than its famed counterpart. The death toll of Jen's new house is startlingly high. Now, she will have to fight to avoid becoming another victim.

"I haven't read all of Andy (Rausch)'s books, but I've read several, and I like that he writes whatever he likes. He's got some damn good stuff." -- Joe R. Lansdale, author of *Bubba Ho-Tep*

"Rausch's writing is like a serpent. It's lean. It's clever. It coils around you…and then it strikes. It's glorious, but be warned—there is no anti-venom." —Chris Miller, author of *Dust*

Madame Gray's Poe-Pourri of Terror"

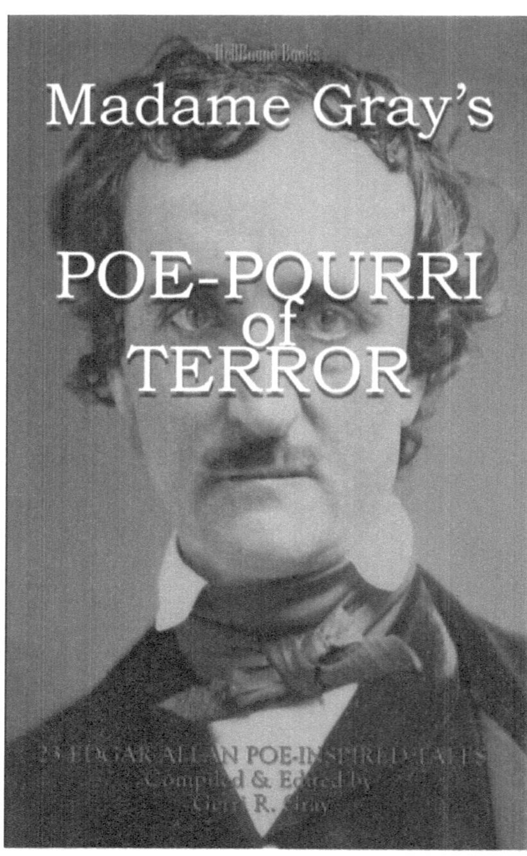

A haunting collection of twenty-three terror-filled tales that pay loving homage to - and capture the very essence of - Edgar Allan Poe.
So, prepare yourself for blood-chilling nightmares as murder, madness, and the supernatural are masterfully blended together to create a delectably wicked potpourri of the macabre.
Featuring exemplary stories of horror from:
R. C. Mulhare, Scot Carpenter, Stephen A. Roddewig, Gerardo Serrano R., Greg Patrick, Drew Nicks, J. Rocky Colavito, Bernardo Villela, James Musgrave, Carlton Herzog, Barbara Jacobson, Guy Riessen, Jane Nightshade, Floyd Mcmillan, Jr., Jeanette Gibson, Bill Camp, J Louis Messina, N.D. Coley, Brett Knepper, Josh Poole, Jameson Grey, and the inimitable Gerri R. Gray.

**A HellBound Books LLC
Publication**

www.hellboundbookspublishing.com